SLEIGHED

VI KEELAND
PENELOPE WARD

SLEIGHED
Cover designer: Sommer Stein, Perfect Pear Creative
Editing: Jessica Royer Ocken
Formatting and proofreading: Elaine York,
Allusion Publishing
Proofreading: Julia Griffis

SLEIGHED

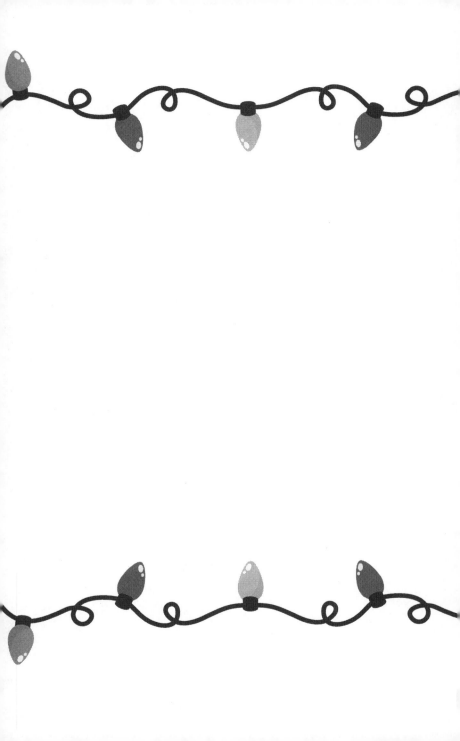

GET SLEIGHED

CHAPTER 1

Sarah

"What are you doing tomorrow?"

My best friend, Jane, had been calling every day since my breakup, trying to get me to go out. But I just wasn't ready yet.

"Anything that doesn't involve men," I said. "I'm pretty sure I've developed an allergy."

"This is most definitely a man-free activity. Can you be at the recording studio at nine?"

"Where are we going?"

"Nowhere. My guest for tomorrow just canceled. I need you to fill in."

Jane was the host of a hugely successful podcast called *Fun with Dick and Jane*. There wasn't actually a cohost named Dick. The title referred to the subject matter of the show—dating *dicks*. I'd been a guest a few times before.

"I don't know how much fun I'll be. What's the topic?"

"Well, my guest was supposed to be Cheri Lord, the woman who just wrapped that reality TV show where your exes get to pick who you should date. Did you see it?"

VI KEELAND & PENELOPE WARD

"No, I didn't, but I saw it advertised."

"You have to watch it. It was a shit show. She cheated on most of her exes, so they all picked serial cheaters and assholes. Anyway, tomorrow's show was billed as 'The Ex Factor — learning from your mistakes.' So you'll be perfect."

I sighed. "Will you come with me to Cabo the day after Christmas if I do it?"

"You know I wish I could. I've never been on a private plane before. But the show has me doing appearances in New York since I'm going to my parents' for Christmas. Trust me, I would much rather be on your fancy vacation than doing that. Every time they make me do these dumb things, at least one creepy guy shows up and just stares at me from the back of the room as I talk. And there's always an old biddy who raises her hand like she wants to ask a question, but then lectures me on improving my language or acting more like a lady on the show. Did you ask Emily if she can go?"

"She's going to Virginia to meet the parents of that new guy she's dating."

I really didn't want to go to Mexico alone, but I also wasn't giving up the amazing trip my ex had bought me for my thirtieth birthday last month—an all-expense-paid vacation for two to Cabo San Lucas, on a private jet with a stay at a five-star hotel that I could never afford, even if I flew coach. When Trent had dumped me two weeks ago, telling me he'd fallen for his *nineteen-year-old* assistant, he'd suggested I take a friend. I was pretty certain the idiot hadn't paid for the trip anyway, probably just put it on his daddy's black card, like everything else in his spoiled life. *Whatever. I'm not bitter or anything...*

"So will you be tomorrow's guest? *Pleeeeease.*"

I really didn't feel like it, but Jane was always there for me. "Sure, no problem."

"Awesome. I'll bring Bloody Marys for breakfast."

The next morning, I arrived at the recording studio a few minutes before nine. Jane kissed my cheek and handed me a cocktail with celery, bacon, and olives sticking out. "Think you can come up with five signs that the new guy you just met is destined to be your ex?" she asked.

I snort laughed. "If I could, I probably wouldn't still be single."

Jane waved me off. "Just make up something that sounds clinical. You're good at sounding smart."

I polished off the last of my Bloody Mary during the ten-second countdown before we were live. Jane opened the show with her usual taglines, and then did a plug for one of her sponsors before introducing me.

"Ladies, I have a treat for you today! The one and only Sarah McGraw is here to discuss all our screwed-up relationships. If you're a new listener and haven't had the pleasure of meeting Sarah yet, let me give you the low-down. Sarah is a graduate of Brown University—summa cum laude, because she's no slouch. She holds a PhD in clinical psychology and is a practicing marriage counselor right here in sunny Los Angeles. More importantly, she's been my best friend since we were four years old and was the *only person* to warn me not to date Tommy Finnegan in high school, even though I did it anyway, and he dumped me *a half hour* after he took my virginity. So please give a warm *Fun with Dick and Jane* welcome to Sarah as she helps us see the warning flags about the men we meet *before* we open up our hearts *and wallets* to them!"

I smiled and spoke into the microphone. "Wow, that's some introduction. Thank you. Tommy Finnegan, huh? That's a name I haven't heard in a long time."

Jane laughed. "He was so damn good looking. Tommy, if you're out there listening—or if any of our listeners know a Tommy Finnegan who graduated from Carnegie High in New York in 2010—I'd love to see a photo of him now."

I shook my head. "Oh my God. People, please do *not* send her a photo, especially if he's still good looking. She's a sucker for guys with dimples."

Jane sighed. "That I am, Sarah. That I am. But as long as we're on the topic, I think Tommy is as good a place as any to start today. You warned me not to go out with him, so I'm guessing you saw a red flag before I did."

"Uh...yeah. He'd dated half the school. His nickname was *Fuck Me Finnegan*. And he took you to see a *porno* on your first date."

"Hey, don't knock it. I learned a lot of useful tricks from that movie."

I laughed. I'd forgotten what a good time Jane and I had on the air. It was pretty much a comedy show for the next forty-five minutes as we talked about Jane's past relationships and the red flags she should have seen, but didn't. After, she opened up the call-in line for questions, and the fun continued.

"Hi, Jane. Hi, Sarah. My name is Megan."

"Hi, Meg!" we said in unison.

"Jane, I just wanted to call in and tell you that Tommy Finnegan breaking up with you a half hour after sex is not the worst breakup. *I* have the worst story. My ex, Jason, dumped me while he was still *inside me*."

My eyes widened. "Oh my."

"That's not the worst part," the caller said. "He also told me he had cancer. He said he didn't know how much time he had left and wanted to be free."

I held my hand over my heart. "Holy crap. He really had cancer?"

"No! The bastard freaking lied."

"Jesus," Jane gasped. "That might be the worst break-up story I've ever heard."

"Sadly, I'm still struggling to get over him. This just happened a month ago. So I wanted to ask Sarah if she has any advice on getting over a guy who doesn't deserve you."

Jane looked at me and smirked. "You go solo to Cabo and sleep with the hottest guy you find?"

I chuckled. "Not happening."

The next few calls were women sharing their horrible breakup stories. One had been dumped at her father's wake, and another said she went to work on a Tuesday morning and her boyfriend moved his stuff out of her house and into the next-door neighbor's. Apparently he'd been sleeping with her for a while. Holy crap, by the time we took a sponsor break, there were more women waiting on hold to share their stories than time left on Jane's show.

She took off her headphones for the short break. "I have a crazy idea..."

"Oh no—I'm not going to get locked out of a window on the thirty-second floor trying to spy on a guy you went on one date with again, am I?"

"No, this is better. Why don't we run a contest on my show: *worst dump story ever*. The winner gets to go to Cabo with you!"

I shook my head. "I don't know...sharing a hotel with a stranger?"

"We go out with men we meet on dating apps. Sharing the penthouse suite of a luxury hotel with a woman is a lot less scary. Plus, you said it had two bedrooms, right? So it's not like you'd be sharing a mattress. I bet I could get one of my sponsors to cover the cost of the winner's trip. It would be a win-win. You'd have a single woman to travel with and a big fat check from one of my sponsors!"

"I don't think so..."

"Don't say no until I hit up my sponsors and see what they're willing to pay, okay? Let's see what we're talking about..."

In a matter of just a few minutes, Jane ended up getting more sponsorship for the contest than she knew what to do with. And now I was officially roped into this.

The podcast was also flooded with so many emails that the staff couldn't keep up with sifting through them. The contest was dubbed "Christmas in Cabo," since the winner and I would be leaving the morning after Christmas.

A week had passed, and today was the big day where we were going to announce the winner live on the air after reading the top three selections. The show had posted ten finalists previously on their website so that listeners could vote for the top three online.

I sat in my seat across from Jane in the studio, anxiously awaiting the results. Not like I was going to meet the winner today, but I was still nervous.

"Okay, folks..." Jane announced. "It's the moment you've all been waiting for. After hundreds of astoundingly horrible—but oh so good—dump stories were submitted, we were able to narrow it down to three. Are you ready, Sarah?"

I pretended to be more excited than I was. "I'm super stoked, yeah. I can't wait to see which one the listeners chose. I have to say, they all have my own dump story beat."

"Okay, without further ado, let's get to it. The second runner-up submission as chosen by our listeners is—drumroll, please!" The sound tech played a rolling drum sound effect as Jane said, "Kate from Irvine! Kate wrote in: 'You could say I was indirectly dumped. My friend was on Tinder and matched with my boyfriend at the time. Not only was he on the dating app, actively cheating on me, but he'd used a photo of the two of us as his profile picture and cut most of me out of it.'"

I cringed and spoke into the mic. "Kate, you are so much better off without him."

Jane continued, "Kate, while you were not the winning submission, we *will* be sending you a consolation package that will include a *Fun with Dick and Jane* T-shirt and matching beer koozie."

"Oooh, I want a beer koozie!" I joked.

"We'll hook you up, too, Sarah." Jane laughed. "Okay, now to our next finalist. The dump story our listeners chose as the first runner-up was submitted by Leela from Riverside, who wrote: 'My father unexpectedly passed away last year. After the burial, my boyfriend texted me that my dad's death had taught him that life was short. He no longer felt it would be fair to string me along when he wasn't in love with me. So not only did I lose my dad, I also lost my boyfriend in the same week. Oh, and my dad had left my ex an expensive watch in his will, thinking he would be my husband sometime soon, and the idiot demanded we actually give it to him.'"

"Oh, Leela. What a jerk," I said into the mic.

"Leela, while you totally deserve a trip to Cabo after dealing with that insensitive loser, again, you are our first runner-up. But the good news is, our producers will be sending you a *Fun with Dick and Jane* self-care package that includes wine, chocolate, and the best in beauty care, thanks to our sponsors. Thank *you* so much for participating, Leela!"

I spoke into the mic. "Enjoy, Leela!"

"And now for the moment we've all been waiting for." Jane paused. "The winner of the 2022 Christmas in Cabo contest. It was a tough one. But this person's dump story seemed to resonate with our listeners the most. Kelly from Burbank. Kelly wrote in with a story that made our blood boil. Kelly writes: 'A few years ago I was dating someone I also worked with, who gave me the impression that they were trustworthy. I told this person about a concept for a unique product I'd come up with. I shouldn't have. Because, not soon after, I was suddenly dumped, and the company we both worked for introduced plans for a new product. It was exactly what I'd shared with the snake who dumped me, down to every last detail. The company went on to make millions off this device, and I got no credit for it, because I'd never patented anything. My ex, however, was promoted.'" Jane paused. "So, Kelly..."

The sound tech introduced some celebratory music.

"Our hearts break for the betrayal you endured. We believe you deserve to take your mind off things for a while. You, my friend, have won the trip to Cabo San Lucas with my girl, Sarah! A limo will pick you up and take you to the airport where you and Sarah will fly via private jet to Cabo San Lucas, Mexico, the morning after Christmas. Should you decide for any reason not to accept this grand prize, the trip will go to our first runner-up, Leela from

Riverside. Our producers have all of your information and will contact you via the email you provided to make the arrangements. A huge congratulations, Kelly! You deserve it after all that!"

"Yay, Kelly!" I clapped, but inside I was beginning to wonder what the hell I'd gotten myself into.

I ended up skipping Christmas with my family this year. With the Cabo trip coming up, it would've been too much to fly to New York and then get back here the next day to catch my plane. And admittedly, there was another reason I was avoiding it: I would've had to endure their questions about my current dating life, and worse, rehash the story of what happened with my ex to those who had no idea we'd even broken up.

The morning after Christmas, I couldn't have been more ambivalent about this whole vacation-with-a-stranger thing. My plan was to enjoy this time alone and not worry about whether this Kelly chick and I got along. We didn't even have to see each other, I suppose. It *was* nice that half of the trip wouldn't be going to waste. But vacationing with a stranger is awkward—plain and simple. I didn't need us to be Thelma and Louise. I just needed to be able to tolerate her in the event she chose to hang out with me and not do her own thing.

The plan was for Kelly to meet me at the airport after the limo dropped her off. They'd let me know the exact spot where they'd be bringing her so I could wait there. I had no idea what to expect; I didn't even know this chick's age. For all I knew, she could have been old enough to be my grandmother or eighteen.

Finally, in the distance, I could see the black limo approaching. Butterflies swarmed in my belly. Okay, maybe I wasn't as ambivalent as I'd thought. It felt like I was The Bachelor, waiting for the limo to pull up and not knowing what the woman exiting the vehicle was going to be like.

When the limo pulled up, no one came around to open the back door. Instead, the door swung open and out came one of the tallest men I'd ever seen. He wore a Hawaiian shirt, a jumbo straw hat, and had what looked like Mardi Gras beads around his neck.

What the hell?

"Please tell me you're Sarah." He smiled.

I had to admit, under that gargantuan hat, he had a pretty gorgeous face and piercing blue eyes.

I cleared my throat. "I am."

Before I could get another word out, I went flying into the air. He'd lifted me up off my feet and spun me around so fast I nearly vomited.

"Dude, this is gonna be awesome," he said as he planted me back on my feet.

Dude? "What? Excuse me. Who are you, and where the hell is Kelly?"

"You're looking at him." He held his hand out. "Kelly Fugger. Great to meet you, Sarah."

"Kelly Fucker?"

"Fugger. F-U-G-G-E-R."

Well, isn't this a bitch... I'm fugged.

CHAPTER 2

Sarah

"How can you be Kelly? You're supposed to be a woman..."

The guy pulled out the waistband of his shorts and peeked inside. "Sorry. Still not a woman. Though I have to admit, it's been a while since I had a reason to check." He shrugged. "I've had a bit of a dry spell since the vibrator thief and I split up."

I blinked a few times. "Vibrator thief?"

He nodded. "That's how I won the contest. My ex, Kelly—"

I interrupted him. "Wait, your name is Kelly *and* your ex's name is Kelly?"

"I know what you're thinking, but she didn't steal my name, too. She was born a month before me."

The lines that had been etched into my forehead since he stepped out of the car deepened. "I'm so confused..."

He nodded. "I felt the same way when I saw Dr. Phil unveiled at our annual new-product presentation."

"Dr. Phil?"

"That's what I'd named the vibrator I'd invented. You know, before Dr. Phil started on *Oprah,* he used to host self-help seminars, and now he's a relationship guru." Kelly shrugged. "Isn't that what a vibrator is? Self-help when you're in a bad relationship? Anyway, the company I work for renamed it Butterfly Kisses or some shit like that, so it's probably why you never heard of Dr. Phil the vibrator."

I rubbed my temples. "Listen, Kelly, I'm not sure where the mix-up occurred, but the contest winner was supposed to be a woman. It wasn't open to men."

He wagged a finger at me. "That's what I initially assumed, but I checked the rules on the website before I entered, and it didn't mention that you had to be a woman."

The stretch limo started to pull away. I raised my hand and yelled, "*Wait!*" But the damn thing kept going.

I shook my head. "Well, I'm sorry the podcast must've forgotten to put that in the rules, but I can't share a hotel room with a man."

"Still haven't forgiven the gender for what your ex did, so you don't want to be around a man, huh?"

"What? *No!* I mean, yes, I'm still angry at my ex, but no, that's not the reason I don't want to share a room with a man."

"So what's the problem?"

"I'm just not comfortable doing that."

"Is it because you're attracted to me?" He pointed to his eyes and fluttered his long, dark lashes. "Some people call these bedroom eyes."

Oh my God. "Listen, Kelly. I'm really sorry for the mix-up. But I'm not going on this trip with you. I was already hesitant about sharing space with a woman. There's just no way I can go with you."

He nodded. "I understand."

"You do?"

Kelly rubbed his bottom lip with his thumb. "What if I get my own room? And just catch a ride with you on the PJ and share the meal and alcohol plan that comes with the hotel stay?"

I shook my head. "I don't know..."

We were still standing out in front of the private-jet terminal. A guy in a uniform walked over. "Ms. McGraw?"

I turned. "Yes?"

"Your flight is ready to board."

"Okay. Can you just...give me one moment, please?"

"Sure. But that's all we have. The air traffic controller is backed up, and if we don't take off in the next fifteen minutes, we're going to lose our spot."

I nodded. "I'll just be a minute."

Kelly lifted a brow. "So what do you say? Am I in?"

I didn't want to go on a trip with this guy, but I felt badly about the mix-up. Plus, how could I say no when he was willing to get a separate room? I took a deep breath and nodded. "Okay, but you need to find your own place to stay."

"Sweet!" An adorable, dimpled smile slid across his face. Kelly grabbed his luggage and motioned to the door with a wide swing of his hand. "Shall we?"

I sighed. "I guess so."

A few minutes later, we were walking side by side on the tarmac, making our way to the plane. "For a second there, I was thinking this wasn't going to happen," he said. "But once I heard your last name, I knew it was fate."

I scrunched up my nose. "My last name?"

"McGraw." He winked. "That's Dr. Phil's last name."

Wow. He cleaned up really nice.

If Kelly hadn't waved and stood up from the table where he was already seated when I walked into the restaurant, I might not have recognized him. He'd shaved the beard he'd been sporting this morning and was now dressed in a jacket and tie. The hotel's restaurants all had a strict dinner dress code. The maître d' walked me over. Kelly stepped around to the chair across from his and pulled it out.

"Thank you." I smiled as I sat. "I almost didn't recognize you without the beard, straw hat, and mismatched Hawaiian clothing. You went from tourist to chic."

He took the seat across from me. "And I almost didn't recognize you smiling."

I bit my lip, embarrassed. "I'm sorry about the way that I acted earlier. I was just caught really off guard."

Kelly laid the napkin over his lap. "It's okay. I get it. I hope you don't mind me saying you look prettier with a smile."

"Thank you."

He looked around. "This place is fancy. How's your room?"

"It's really nice. How about yours? Were you able to get a room at the place next door the front desk recommended?" Unfortunately, the hotel where I was staying was booked solid.

"No, they were sold out. Most places were. I'm a few blocks over at a motel. They only had a room available for five of the six nights, but I'll find someplace to stay the last night."

I'd thought a lot about how I'd made Kelly go somewhere else, as I lay poolside being served piña coladas this afternoon. While I didn't think I should've had to share a room with him, it was wrong of me to not offer to cover the cost. I'd made a boatload off the contest from Jane's sponsors.

"I'd like to pay the cost of your hotel room. You won a contest fair and square, so you shouldn't have to pay for any of the trip amenities that were promised to you."

Kelly waved me off. "It's okay. It's not that expensive, which is fair considering the rats."

My eyes widened.

Kelly grinned. "I'm joking."

I chuckled. "Thank God. It's hard to tell when you're kidding. Like this afternoon, were you serious about inventing...you know, Dr. Phil?"

"I don't joke about vibrators," he deadpanned.

"Oh..."

He smirked. "I'm teasing. But to answer your question, yes, I did invent Dr. Phil. I'm a product developer for Lucy Goosey Couples Toys."

The waiter came over with a basket of tortilla chips and guacamole and asked to take our wine order. I told Kelly I wasn't picky, and he proceeded to speak to the waiter in fluent Spanish, without even needing to look at the menu.

"Wow, did you just order wine?" I asked when the waiter walked away.

He nodded. "A merlot. I read an article on the plane about a local winemaker, so I asked the waiter if they carried it." Kelly held the basket out to me to take a chip before taking one for himself. "You know, because my travel buddy wouldn't speak to me during the entire flight."

"Sorry about that, too. Luckily, the piña coladas I had after we arrived helped me climb down off my high horse."

"It's fine. I'm just messing with you again." He dipped his chip into the guac. "So tell me, are you really a marriage counselor, or was that just a bit for the show?"

"No, I'm actually a marriage counselor."

"What's that like?"

"Well, there's never a dull moment, that's for sure. One minute I'll have a couple in my office crying, and the next minute a couple will be screaming at the top of their lungs."

"Yeah, my business is the same. Some testers cry, some scream for joy."

I started to smile, then stopped. "Joking, right?"

"Yes, indeedy."

"So how did you get into your line of work?"

"Engineering degree from MIT, of course."

"I can't tell if you're kidding or not?"

"I'm serious. I went to school for engineering, then did a stint as a developer for a robotics company. I was bored to death. Saw an ad for a job making women's products, and I applied, half as a joke. Seven years later, I'm still there."

"So you like your job, then?"

"Mostly I enjoy the human-testing phase where I get to try the products out on people."

My eyes grew wide.

Kelly's blue eyes sparkled as he leaned in. "Breathe. I'm joking. There is a human-testing phase, but we just read their written feedback."

That was pretty much how the next two hours went. Kelly entertained me with his dry sense of humor while we drank two bottles of delicious local wine. I couldn't remember a time when I'd laughed so much on a first date, except...this wasn't a date. After dinner, Kelly walked me to the elevator.

"What time do you want to meet for breakfast?"

"Is nine too late? Service ends at ten."

"Works for me. 'Night, Sarah."

"Goodnight, Kelly."

Back in my room, I washed off my makeup and changed for bed. Even though wine usually made me sleepy, I felt a little wired as I slipped beneath the covers. I was also feeling a little *needy*. It must've been all that talk about vibrators. So I got back out of bed and went to the hidden pocket in my suitcase to grab the little toy I'd brought with me. It took all of three minutes to get myself off. When I was done, I set my pink vibrator on the end table and reached up to turn the light off. But something on the bottom of the toy caught my eye. It looked like a logo with two script letters entwined, and if I wasn't mistaken, the letters were *LG*. I lifted it for a closer inspection—sure enough, the manufacturer name stamped onto the bottom of the logo was listed as *Lucy Goosey*.

Oh my God.

Was it possible that my tripmate was responsible for the orgasm I'd just had?

CHAPTER 3

Kelly

Sarah was already seated, with a heaping plate from the buffet, when I spotted her in the restaurant. I headed straight for her table and slid into the seat across from her.

"Aren't you gonna get food?" she asked with her mouth full. "I'm sorry—I was too hungry to wait."

"I'll get something in a minute. I want to ask you something first."

"What's up?"

Filled with adrenaline, I wriggled my brows. "Feel like going on a little excursion today?"

"Depends."

"Do you have plans?" I asked.

She wiped her mouth with a napkin. "I booked an appointment at the spa for noon, actually."

"Cancel it. I have something better."

Sarah shook her head and sipped her coffee. "I don't know what could be much better than a deep-tissue massage, but I'm listening."

Stealing one of the grapes off the side of her plate, I chewed and said, "I rented an ATV to tour the beach. It's the best way to see everything. It's got two seats, so what a waste if I don't have anyone to go with me."

She bit her bottom lip and seemed to be considering my offer.

"Come on," I prodded. "The spa will still be here tomorrow. But I could only get the ATV for today. They were booked the rest of the week."

"Okay, then." She shrugged. "Yeah. I'll go."

"Sweet." I smiled before getting up to head to the buffet. "Be right back."

Now I felt like I could relax and eat. For some reason, I'd been anxious to ask her to go with me. While Sarah had seemed pretty standoffish when we first met, she now seemed a bit more open to actually hanging out and having fun on her vacation. So at least there was hope. I certainly hadn't come on this trip expecting to be attracted to my travel mate. In fact, I'd had no expectations about anything at all. I'd been bored one day on my lunch break, fucking around when I entered that contest. I never in a million years thought I'd actually win the damn thing. Which is probably why I didn't take things seriously at first. Case in point, I'd worn that get-up to the airport to be funny. Of course, Sarah thought I was a lunatic. Turns out, she was only half-right.

After picking up the ATV and gearing up in our helmets, we took off and explored the beautiful white-sand beach, basking in the bright sunshine while waves crashed in the distance. I didn't mind having her arms wrapped around me one bit. It was hard to hear each other while we were riding, though, so we had to speak loudly.

"So what happened with your ex?" I shouted as we rode along the beach.

"You want me to talk about that now, when we're supposed to be having fun?"

"Why not? That way we can get all the downer stuff over with. Would you rather tell me about it over dinner when you can hear a pin drop?"

She shouted over the motor. "Okay...my ex, Trent, who I'd been with since college, left me for his nineteen-year-old assistant. That's all there is to it. Happy now? He traded me in for a new model."

"You know what they say when it comes to newer models versus the original?" I yelled.

"What's that?"

"They don't make 'em like they used to. Cheaper parts. Anyway, you're a smoke show, Sarah. He's smoking crack."

"Well, thank you." She held onto me tighter. "You know, it kind of felt good yelling everything out."

"Really? Do it some more."

"What do you mean?"

"Yell out your frustrations!"

I didn't think she was going to take me up on that until I heard her scream behind me at the top of her lungs.

"Fuck you, Trent!"

"There you go!" I said, revving the engine and going a bit faster. "He's missing out on a damn good time here, too. Suits him right."

We rode along without talking for a bit.

"Your turn," she said. "I know a little about your dump story. You said her name was Kelly. What was so special about that vibrator anyway?"

"The clit tickler," I yelled.

"What?"

"Did you not hear me? Or do you just want to hear me say it again?"

"I heard you. I guess I couldn't believe my ears."

"Clit tickler!" I yelled even louder. "Say it again for the people in the back. Clit tickler!"

She was laughing hysterically. "Please explain."

"I don't know how comfortable you are with this stuff."

"Do you think I'm some kind of prude? I'll have you know, I actually own a Lucy Goosey vibrator."

"Oh man. Do you happen to have the make and model number?"

"Why?"

"I want to know if I had anything to do with the design."

"I can let you know." She squeezed my side. "Anyway, tell me about this clit-tickler thing. How did it come about?"

"Well, as you know, my ex also worked for the company. One night I was...going down on her. And she said, 'Damn, you're so good at that. You should patent it.' I asked her to be more specific. She said it was the precise way I tickled her with my tongue. So I started designing this contraption that would attach to the vibrator and apply just the right amount of pressure on a woman's clit. The idea of a clit tickler was nothing new. But it was the specific mechanism and speed options of the one attached to Dr. Phil that made it special—that and the warm lubricant dispenser."

"How could she do that to you?"

"Very easily. She's an asshole, number one. Number two, we had detailed discussions about it, so I made it easy, I guess. Because all of our conversations were verbal, I had no way of proving she wasn't the one who'd initiated the design."

"Fuck you, clit-tickler-stealing bitch!" she screamed.

"Nice!" I laughed. "I like it when you're angry."

"Would you be offended if I bought Dr. Phil, though? You know, to see firsthand what you're talking about?"

"Butterfly Kisses, it's officially called. And not at all. I absolve you of any guilt."

Sarah and I had a really good time on the ATV ride, but I didn't want to push my luck with her. So after we returned our vehicle, I told her I was heading back to my motel.

"Would you want to join me for dinner?" she asked.

I acted casual. "Yeah, I mean, if you want the company."

"It would be nice not to eat alone."

"That's the only reason you want me there, so you don't have to look pathetic?"

"No. I want you there because I enjoy your company," she admitted.

"Okay then." I grinned. "Why don't I go back, shower and change, and I'll meet you at La Casa at seven."

She smiled. "Sounds good."

Five margaritas in, Sarah was shitfaced. Let's just say, she asked if I wanted to dance—even though there was no music or dance floor in this place. It was all good, though. This lady needed to unwind. After talking further at dinner, I learned she was more deeply scarred by her breakup than I'd thought. It had done a number on her self-esteem and made me want to kill that fucker for making her think she was less than she was, when in reality *he* was the insecure one.

I got the impression that she felt sorry for me because of what happened with my ex stealing my idea. I never wanted to come across as braggy, so I didn't flaunt my wealth. Even though I didn't get credit for Dr. Phil, I'd made millions by going on to create a number of novel adult products that did very well. I now also owned a decent amount of stock in the company. Basically, I was shacking up at the motel down the road when I could've funded this vacation for both of us many times over. I hadn't taken the trip for the free ride. It was about the blind adventure for me.

"Can you walk me back to my room?" she asked.

I paused, unsure if she was suggesting *more* than just a walk. "Of course. I wouldn't let you walk back alone this late."

There was a mellow breeze as we meandered back to Sarah's suite. I wanted to see her all the way to the door since she was too drunk to be trusted to find her room.

When we finally got there, she looked at me hazily. "Would you want to come in?"

It didn't take a rocket scientist to know that if I went in, there was a damn good chance something might happen between us. And damn, did I ever want it to. This girl was so hot, smart, funny—but vulnerable. And as I'd learned from talking to her tonight...special. She was real. As real as my dick was hard right now. But unfortunately, she was also drunk as a skunk. And I would never take advantage of her under these conditions.

"I'll tell you what..." I said. "I'm not gonna come in right now. Because you're really drunk. But if you still want me to come *visit* in the morning when you're clear headed, I'm down. You just let me know."

She snorted. "You think I'm trying to get in your pants?"

"I didn't say that. I just said you're drunk, and it's better if I don't come in."

She pointed into my chest with her index finger. "I'm not...trying...to...get...in...your pants." She stumbled. "You're not even my type."

"Oh really? What's your type?"

"Uglier men than you, typically." She snorted.

"That's very offensive," I joked.

"Well, then you're easily offended."

"That I am definitely not. I'm a huge dude named Kelly, my last name is Fugger, and I design dicks for a living. Definitely not easily offended."

She giggled. "Anyway, don't need you to come in anyway. I have my Lucy Goosey toy tonight, thanks to you, Fucker." She hiccupped. "Fugger. Fucker. Whatever."

"Alright, drunky." I laughed. "Go have fun with your Lucy Goosey. Get some sleep. I'll see you tomorrow?" I reached down and kissed her forehead.

She smiled up at me and hiccupped again. "'Night, Clit-Tickler Fucker Fugger."

CHAPTER 4

Kelly

The following morning, Sarah didn't show up for breakfast. I was disappointed, but figured she might have had a bit of a hangover and slept in. When lunchtime rolled around, I went back to her hotel even though I wasn't hungry, hoping maybe she'd make it for the next meal. But after two hours of sitting in the lobby outside the restaurant that served lunch trying to look casual, it was clear she wasn't coming again. I did a quick sweep around the pool and beach, thinking perhaps she'd just ordered room service and was now basking in the sun. But Sarah was nowhere to be found. It made me a little worried, so I decided to call her room from one of the hotel phones before I left to make sure she was okay.

"Hello?" a hoarse voice answered. I wasn't even sure I'd reached the right room, the person sounded so terrible.

"Sarah?"

"Yeah?"

"It's Kelly. Are you okay?"

"Not really. I've been throwing up since the middle of the night. And, well, let's just say that's not the only way things are exiting my body."

"Ah. Not fun. I noticed last night that you ordered the first two margaritas on the rocks before you switched to the frosted ones. You think the ice got you?"

"Maybe." She sighed. "I'd been so careful. But tequila makes me stupid, and apparently I'm paying for it now."

"What can I do to help?"

"Nothing really. I think it's mostly run its course. There's not much left in my stomach for my body to reject. Now my head is just pounding, which is probably because I'm so dehydrated."

"There's a grocery store down the road. I'll go grab you some supplies and leave them at your door."

"You don't have to do that."

"I want to. Give me about ten minutes. I'll knock to let you know when they're there, and you can open after I leave so you have your privacy."

"Okay, thank you."

The trip for supplies took longer than I expected. I wound up going to two stores since the first one didn't have everything I needed. When I arrived at Sarah's door, I set the bag down and lightly knocked. I started to walk away, but her door opened.

I turned. "How you feeling?"

She smiled halfheartedly. "As good as I look."

Sarah's hair was disheveled, her skin was pale, and she didn't have an ounce of makeup on, but she was still absolutely gorgeous. "If you feel as good as you look, then let's go ziplining, because even sickly you're more beautiful than any woman in this hotel."

She blushed. "That's sweet of you, even if it's not true. Would you...want to come in and hang out? I don't think what I have is contagious..."

I had actually made a reservation to go ziplining, but if my choices were an adventure in the jungle or holding Sarah's hair back while she puked, sadly, I'd rather play ponytail holder. "Sure, if you're up for it."

She opened the door and stepped aside, and I whistled when I got a look at her suite. "So this is how the other half lives? The cockroaches in my place kept me up half the night singing 'La Cucaracha.'"

"Please tell me you're joking."

"I'm joking."

"Thank God."

"They were actually singing 'La Bamba.'"

Sarah smiled and pointed to the bag in my arms. "If you don't have Gatorade in that bag, I can't promise the next time I puke it won't be on you."

I reached into the bag and pulled out a red Gatorade. "Even though the alternative is so tempting..."

We sat down on the couch in the living room. Sarah chugged electrolytes while I unloaded the rest of my custom-made Mexican-hangover/Montezuma's-revenge kit. I held each item out to her like I was Vanna White.

Pepto Bismol – "Fun fact," I said. "There's no medicinal reason it's pink. The manufacturer adds the color to make it more appealing to children."

Saltines – "It's less about the cracker and more about the salt. It helps you retain water when you're dehydrated."

Ginger Ale – "Settles the belly."

A giant orange – "Vitamin C."

27

The last item on the bottom of the bag was a movie-theatre-sized box of Red Hots. Sarah's nose wrinkled. "Those cure an upset stomach?"

"Nope, these are for me. I love these damn things. I like to shove a whole handful into my mouth so my eyes water."

Sarah laughed. "Thank you for doing all this."

"No problemo."

"I hope I wasn't too obnoxious last night. I'm normally a two-glasses-of-wine-max drinker. Maybe three on Christmas when I'm with my entire family. I guess since I skipped Christmas this year, I made up for the lost alcohol by drinking five at once."

"Nah, you were fun. But what do you mean you skipped Christmas?"

"My parents are super festive—Christmas sweaters with bells and all." She shrugged. "I just didn't feel much in the mood to celebrate, so I lied and told them my flight got canceled at the last minute."

"What did you do on the big day?"

"I stayed home in my pajamas and ate a frozen Lean Cuisine. I think it might've been the first time in my thirty years that I didn't open a single present on Christmas."

"That sounds...sad."

She chuckled. "It was. I don't recommend it." Sarah cracked the top of the Pepto bottle open and chugged from the plastic. "What did you do for Christmas this year?"

"My family's pretty small. It's just me, my mom, and my uncle, Jimmy. Mom is super religious, so I took them to midnight mass on Christmas Eve. I sleep over at her house on Christmas Eve every year because the thing that makes her the happiest in the world is putting presents under the tree after I fall asleep and waking up to open them all together."

"Awww... That's so sweet."

"Yeah, my mom thinks so. But that's mostly because she has no idea that I slip Uncle Jimmy his real gift without her seeing."

"Which is..."

"Weed and German porn."

"Seriously?"

"Yep. He looks forward to his one joint and 1950's-era German pornography all year. It's become sort of a silent tradition, ever since I stumbled onto his collection during a visit when I was eighteen."

She laughed. "That's so funny."

"Not to Uncle Jimmy. He takes his porn stash very seriously."

Over the next few hours we wound up talking about our favorite Christmas memories. I told Sarah about the year my mom woke me and my sister up at the crack of dawn, put us both in the car in our pajamas, and drove us to the airport for a surprise trip to Disney. It was my happiest Christmas, until I realized the vacation had been my sister Elizabeth's Make-A-Wish trip, and it meant she'd be gone a few months later. She'd had terminal leukemia. Sarah told me about the boy next door whom she'd had a crush on from the time she was ten, but he was four years older. And how at eighteen she'd tricked him into standing under the mistletoe. Then when he went to kiss her cheek, she turned her head and slipped him the tongue.

By the time we came to a lull in our conversation, it was already dark outside.

"Oh my God. What time is it?" Sarah asked. "We've been sitting here rambling all day."

I looked at my phone and realized it was also the first time I'd touched it all day. "It's almost eight."

"I monopolized your entire day sitting here talking about Christmas. You could have been outside enjoying the sunshine."

"It's okay. I like talking to you."

She smiled shyly. "I like talking to you, too. Even though all of our talking about Christmas made me realize I was an idiot for skipping Christmas this year. It's going to be a long three-hundred-and-sixty-two days until the next one."

That gave me an idea. "Why wait that long? There are no rules about when we celebrate the holiday."

"What do you mean?"

"There's a giant tree in the lobby. I think we should have your missed Christmas tomorrow night. We can even make it fun and grab some cheap presents."

Sarah's face lit up. "You're totally getting these wooden cockroaches I saw a guy carving on the street."

I laughed. "Okay, but I'm warning you, I actually know all the words to 'La Cucaracha'. My Spanish teacher, Ms. Chiesa, used to make us all sing it every year. If I get those, expect to be hearing it."

CHAPTER 5

Sarah

Kelly and I agreed to meet at 4 PM by the giant tree in the hotel lobby. The plan was to exchange gifts down there, then go out to dinner. I was definitely getting in the post-Christmas spirit.

One of the best parts about celebrating Christmas after the holiday? Clearance. I'd asked the manager of the place I was staying for a recommendation on where to get after-Christmas stuff, and he'd ordered a car to take me to this small plaza of shops. After browsing a few different stores for something to wear, I was able to find the perfect ugly Christmas sweater, for a great bargain. Since it was hot, I'd wear it inside the hotel only and take it off before dinner. And not only had I picked up the wooden cockroaches from the street vendor for Kelly, but I found him another special surprise gag gift as well.

I couldn't remember the last time I was this excited about "Christmas." Maybe the key was to celebrate away from my family, after the actual holiday, with a handsome stranger. Perhaps this needed to be a yearly tradition. Although I doubted I'd meet anyone by chance again as interesting as Kelly.

Once I got back from shopping, I had about an hour to get ready. Before heading downstairs, I put on a red mini skirt that matched my sweater.

I was so excited to see what Kelly had in store for me. I was a few minutes early, so I stood by the tall Christmas tree and waited, holding the gift bag.

When I turned around, I spotted big, larger-than-life Kelly walking toward me wearing...*what the heck was that*? I soon realized it was a hat with Santa's legs at the top. It was made to look like Santa's feet were sticking up in the air as he got stuck in the chimney, which in this case was Kelly's head. How bizarre—but totally Kelly.

"Nice hat."

"Thanks. I looked everywhere for a Buddy the Elf costume, but no luck."

"I'm so glad you didn't find one." I chuckled.

"That would've been awesome, though. You have to admit." He looked down at my sweater, adorned with embroidered cats in winter hats. "Nice sweater. I love it."

"It was the ugliest sweater I could find. I'm taking it off for dinner, though. It's too hot."

"Taking it off is even better." He smiled mischievously.

I blew out a breath of air, burning up. "Shall we sit to open our presents?"

He placed his hands on my shoulders. "First off, Merry Christmas."

A shiver ran down my spine from the contact. "Merry Christmas to you, Kelly."

"I think we should wait to open the presents, actually," he said.

I looked around. "Wait for what? What else is there?"

I noticed he was carrying a black backpack, which he now removed from his shoulder.

"You can't have a Christmas party without music and appetizers, Sarah."

He pulled a Santa Claus statue of some kind out of his bag. He pressed a button on its feet before placing it on the ground next to us. Santa began swaying his hips to the tune of "Rockin' Around the Christmas Tree."

"You could've just played music on your phone, but he's adorable."

"Music from my phone wouldn't have been as embarrassing. It's more fun to watch your face turn red right now."

Next, he took out some Christmas cookies in a plastic container that looked like they'd come from the supermarket bakery sale section.

Last, he removed two red Solo cups from the bag and a carton of eggnog before pouring us each a glass.

"I'm glad you came prepared," I said.

We sat there with our battery-operated Santa playing music and sipped our eggnog while munching on cookies. Despite being too hot, this was my favorite Christmas in a very long time.

"Present time!" Kelly announced.

I put my cup down and clapped my hands. "I'll go first," I said. I handed him the gift bag, which had little Christmas trees all over it.

"Should I be afraid?" he asked.

I giggled.

He ripped open the first box, and his eyes widened as he lifted the two wooden cockroaches. "I see you're a woman of your word."

"How could I *not* get these for you?"

"By the way, last night, they serenaded me with 'Feliz Navidad'."

I cackled.

"I love them. And they'll always remind me of this trip." He smiled. "Also, I'll spare you my rendition of 'La Cucaracha'."

I pointed. "There's something else in the bag."

Kelly looked down. "Oh yeah." He reached in and opened the second package.

When he saw what was inside, his jaw dropped. He took them out and began shaking them around. "My life is now complete. Who knew there was such a thing as penis maracas?"

These maracas had dicks for handles and big testicles for shakers.

"Given your line of work, I figured those are perfect."

"Hell yeah. These babies are going right on my desk at the office."

"Cool." I laughed and took a deep breath, anticipating what kind of crazy thing he'd bought for me.

"I got you something, too." He smiled.

"I figured."

Kelly reached into his backpack and took out a small, wrapped box. He handed it to me. Seeming a little nervous, he licked his lips as he waited for me to open it.

Is something going to jump out at me?

When I opened the box, my mouth fell open. "Kelly..."

It was the most gorgeous jade pendant—a green, oval stone, surrounded by small diamonds.

"This is... It's beautiful." I looked up at him. "This isn't real, is it? The diamonds and all?"

"Everything is real, yeah," he said.

My eyes widened. "Kelly...why did you do this? We were supposed to give each other gag gifts. I—"

"I wanted to. And I didn't think there were any rules."

"This is too much," I stuttered. "I can't take it."

"Well, you'd better, because I'm not taking it back."

Wow. "It's..." I sighed.

"Look, you hosted me on this vacation. And I wanted to give you something to remember me by." He winked. "After all, that jade is *Kelly* green."

"It's truly beautiful." I rubbed my finger over the stone. "Will you help me put it on?"

"Of course."

I lifted my hair as he took the gorgeous piece and placed it around my neck.

I fondled the chain. "I'll always cherish this. Thank you."

"You're welcome." He beamed.

Kelly had already made me feel special tonight, and we ended up having an amazing dinner after our little Christmas party. We continued to chat, and I loved how self-deprecating he was, despite the fact that he was also quite successful, as I'd come to learn. And he was a damn good person. Even after his ex burned him, he'd still found it in his heart to forgive her. He understood that holding on to toxic resentment was worse for him than anything else. He was wise and offered a perspective I knew I would take home with me. Actually, I started really hoping this didn't have to be the end for us. But at the same time, I knew I wasn't over what had happened with Trent, and I didn't want to lead Kelly on if I wasn't ready to start anything. But did Kelly even want something with me? He hadn't been all that forward, so I wasn't sure.

After our dinner, he walked me back to my room. I'd done something earlier that I hoped wouldn't backfire now. I was about to find out.

We arrived at my door, and he looked up at the mistletoe I'd hung earlier.

"Well, well...what do we have here?" I said.

"That looks like a mistletoe to me." He grinned.

"Indeed, it is."

Adrenaline pumped through me. I reached up, wrapping my hand around the back of his neck, and stood up on my tiptoes. Thankfully, he lowered his beautiful face down to me. When our lips met, I realized how much I'd been starving for this. I slipped him the tongue and heard him laugh under his breath.

He spoke over my lips. "She strikes again."

He was right, but this time, it was so much sweeter.

Our kiss grew more intense as Kelly took the reins, pushing his tongue deeper inside my mouth. He tasted so damn good. I felt my panties getting wet and knew I had a choice to make. I could open the door and pull him inside, or open the door and say goodbye. In the end, fear won out over passion.

I pulled away and suddenly said, "Goodnight, Fugger."

His mouth opened and closed a few times. "Okay...uh, goodnight."

I used my key and slipped inside my room. Leaning my back against the door, I panted as my heart raced, my body still aching for Kelly.

CHAPTER 6

Sarah

I slept like shit.

Not only was I chock full of pent-up frustrations after the amazing kiss with Kelly last night, but I also felt terrible about how I'd pushed him away. He'd been nothing but kind to me—taking me out on an ATV tour, nursing me when I was sick, and then last night he'd given me a gorgeous, expensive necklace. And what had I done in return? Let's see... I'd refused to share my beautiful suite that he'd rightfully won, bought him cockroaches as a gift, and to top it off, I'd dragged him under the mistletoe for a kiss and promptly ran away like he'd given me something contagious.

This morning, I also felt panicky that our trip was coming to an end. I decided I needed to pull up my big-girl panties and lay my cards on the table—tell Kelly I liked him and thought maybe there was something there, but that I was nervous about jumping into something so soon after my breakup. I hoped maybe he'd be okay taking things slow. But when I called to ask if he wanted to meet for breakfast so we could talk, he didn't answer. By lunchtime, I still hadn't heard from him, even though I'd left a message. Finally at two in the afternoon, my phone buzzed. Seeing Kelly's name flash on my screen, I breathed a sigh of relief.

"Hey. I was starting to get worried," I said. "It's not like you to skip a meal."

"I grabbed a muffin at my hotel before I went to find a place to stay tomorrow night."

I'd forgotten the hotel where he was staying didn't have a room available for the last night of our trip. "Did you have any luck?"

"Not anywhere around here. Every hotel on this side of the island is sold out. I found something about a half hour away, though. Before I booked it, I called the hotel you're staying at and asked if anything opened up. They said they might have a room for me, but they won't know until tomorrow morning. Apparently, a guest had a family emergency of some type and is trying to get a flight out, which would leave a vacancy. So I figured I'd wait on booking a place on the other side of town, since they seemed to have plenty of rooms there."

"Oh, wow. It would be great if you could get a room here."

"Yeah. Tell me about it. The walk to a hotel with blue balls kind of sucks." Kelly laughed. "Less chafing if I can move closer."

"About that..."

"It's fine. I'm just teasing you."

"It's not fine. I was actually looking for you earlier, hoping we could talk about last night—about the kiss, I mean. What are you doing right now?"

"I was thinking about going for a swim. It's hot as hell today."

"Would you want to do that over here at my hotel? We could have piña coladas poolside, my treat?"

"Will you wear the white bikini you had hanging in your bathroom when you weren't feeling well the other day?"

"The white thong?"

"That's the one."

"Sure, if you want."

"You can't see me, but I just fist pumped."

I laughed. I could totally visualize the fist pumping. "Meet you in the lobby in a half hour?"

"Sounds good."

Even though I was going to the pool, I put on a full face of makeup. I also heated up my curling iron and made some loose waves in my hair before slipping into the white bikini. I tied a sheer white sarong around my waist and added a big straw hat and sunglasses to complete my ensemble. Checking myself out in the mirror, I thought I looked pretty good. That gave me the confidence I needed as I made my way down to the lobby to meet Kelly. But my outfit wasn't powerful enough to stop the nervous jitters that swarmed in my belly when the doors slid open at the lobby level. I was anxious and excited and...

What the...

I froze midstep getting off the elevator.

What the actual hell?

I blinked a few times, certain I had to be imagining my ex standing at the front desk. But no such luck. That man was definitely Trent.

The elevator car doors tried to close, but I was still standing halfway in and halfway out. So when they hit me, they bounced back open. The woman working behind the desk heard the sound and looked up. Noticing the shocked look on my face, her brows drew together, and Trent turned to follow her line of sight.

A smile spread across his annoyingly handsome face. "There she is…"

"What—what are you doing here?" I shook my head.

"I came to grovel and get my girl back."

A few feet behind him, the lobby door swung open and Kelly strolled in. He took one look at me and whistled. "Wow. My girl looks *smokin'* hot today."

Trent's eyes jumped back and forth between Kelly and me before scanning the rest of the lobby. He seemed to be looking for another person, anyone other than me that Kelly could've been talking to. But we were the only three in the lobby, so it was pretty damn obvious. His eyes narrowed. "Who the hell are you, and why are you calling *my girl your girl?*"

I walked over to Kelly first and quickly explained who Trent was.

"*This* is what you wanted to talk to me about?" Kelly folded his arms across his chest.

I shook my head. "No, no—not at all. I had no idea he was coming when we spoke a little while ago."

"Who the hell is this clown?" Trent thumbed at Kelly.

"This is…Kelly. He won your half of the trip."

"*Won* my half of the trip? What are you talking about?"

"It's a long story, but Jane ran a contest on her podcast, and the winner got to join me on the trip."

"You auctioned off my spot on our vacation for a date?"

"No, no. It's nothing like that. It's not a date."

Kelly frowned. "That kiss at the end of the night last night sure felt a hell of a lot like a date."

Trent scowled. "You kissed this joker?"

Kelly took steps toward Trent. "Who you calling a joker?"

Oh shit. This was about to turn ugly. I stepped between the two men and put my arms out to keep distance between them.

"Kelly, I had no idea Trent was coming. Would you mind if we skipped the pool so he and I can talk?"

Kelly frowned and shook his head. "Whatever. I'll see you around." He turned and stormed out the lobby door. Watching him walk away upset caused a lump to form in my throat. So I ran after him. "Wait! Kelly!" But he was already marching across the parking lot and didn't turn back.

Trent followed me outside. "Sarah, what the hell is going on?"

CHAPTER 7

Kelly

Maybe I overreacted.

I shouldn't have left her alone with him. But then again...she sent me away instead of telling me to stay, so alone time with him was what she'd apparently wanted.

Sitting at a bar by the beach not far from my motel, I read the text from her again.

> Sarah: I'm so sorry my ex showed up. I had no idea he was planning on coming here. I felt like I needed to hear him out. I'm sorry he ruined our plans and you left upset.

I didn't respond. A full hour passed, and I came to the conclusion that if she hadn't reached out to tell me he was gone by now, maybe her asshole ex was getting his message through to her. But it was killing me to sit here and do nothing, so I finally texted her back.

> Kelly: Look, Sarah, I don't know your ex from Adam, but what I do know? You deserve better than that guy.

I don't know what he's saying to you right now, and I don't give a fuck what he has to say. Not everyone deserves a second chance, especially lying, cheating bastards. I've said my piece.

She didn't respond. Another hour went by, and I decided to go back to my room and figure out an exit plan. The more time that passed, the more I started to feel like she might be taking him back. And that sucked. Because I was really starting to like her and had a different idea of how this trip might have ended. For a while there, I'd believed I'd won more than a trip—it'd felt like I'd won the lottery. And now it felt like it was all a freaking dream.

My phone rang. My pulse raced for a second because I thought it was her, but unfortunately, it wasn't. It was a call from Sarah's hotel.

"Mr. Fugger?" a woman said.

"Yes."

"This is Vanessa from the resort hotel?"

"Hi."

"This is a courtesy call to let you know that the room I mentioned to you earlier, the one we thought might become available tomorrow night, is in fact going to remain occupied. The situation with the occupants' family emergency changed, so they've decided to stay through the remainder of their trip after all."

"Great," I muttered. "Well, thank you for letting me know."

I hung up and pulled on my hair. *What now?*

If I wasn't going to have a place to stay tomorrow night, I needed to book myself a flight for tomorrow. I didn't want to stay here anyway if Sarah's "boyfriend" would be sticking around.

I opened my laptop to check flights. There was only one plane out in the morning and a couple more at night. I called the airline. That 10 AM flight was full. They told me they could put me on standby if I wanted to just come to the airport, so that's what I decided to do. Given that Sarah still hadn't contacted me, I was at peace with the decision to leave. Her silence spoke volumes.

The following morning, I was all packed up but felt my walls breaking down a bit. My original plan had been to leave quietly, with little fanfare. But a part of me couldn't do that without seeing her face one last time. I owed her at least a proper goodbye after the time we'd had together, despite my bitterness over her not texting me back.

I decided to have breakfast at the restaurant in her hotel. It would be her call if she wanted to join me. When I got there, I texted her. If she didn't text back this time, it would be the last time I ever reached out.

> Kelly: Hey. Not sure if you're still sleeping or what. But wanted to let you know I'm here at the restaurant for a quick breakfast before I head to the airport this morning. I'm leaving soon, if you're around to say goodbye.

Not even two seconds went by before a response came in.

> Sarah: Goodbye? What do you mean?

> Kelly: I had to check out of my hotel, and the room at yours didn't pan out. Between that and your original

vacation partner showing up, I thought it was best I head out early. My flight leaves at 10 AM.

Sarah: Your flight? Oh my God! Don't you dare leave! I'm coming right down.

Confused, I sat at a table and waited.

The next thing I knew, Sarah was running into the restaurant—in a short, white bathrobe.

I couldn't help but laugh as I stood up from the table. "You could've gotten dressed."

She fastened the tie around her robe. "You were really going to take off?"

"You never texted me back last night. What did you expect?"

"Not this!" She sighed. "Trent wouldn't leave. We spent hours going back and forth—mostly him trying to make excuses for what he did and explaining why I should take him back. It was torture. By the time he finally gave up and realized I wasn't letting him stay with me, it was so late that I decided to just contact you this morning. But you beat me to it."

My eyes narrowed. "Where is he?"

"He went back to the airport late last night."

"He's gone?"

"Yes. I sent him packing. I'm never taking him back after what he did to me. Never."

Relief washed over me. "Well, good."

"He asked me to explain what was going on between you and me. I told him the truth: that, sure, you were a contest winner, but that you turned out to be so much more." She inched toward me. "Kelly, in the short time we've known each other, you've taught me that life is too short to waste time with anyone who doesn't appreciate me. The last thing I told Trent was that I would send him one of your clit ticklers so he could give it to the next poor woman he screws over, because she's going to need it when he leaves her high and dry. He looked at me like I was crazy, but I didn't care." She laughed, then said, "I realize now I should have texted you last night to tell you all this. I never imagined you would have tried to take off so soon."

"I thought you were...with him. I didn't want to stick around for all that."

"No." She shook her head. "All I've wanted this entire time was to get back to you—to get back to that moment where you and I were going to have piña coladas at the pool. I'm so sorry that never happened."

I took a step closer. "You'd said you needed to talk to me yesterday—before he showed up. What was that about?"

"I was going to ask you to spend tonight with me. In my room. In *our* room. The room that was rightfully yours from the beginning."

My heart sped up as I cradled her cheek. "You sure that's what you want?"

"I've never been more sure of anything."

Letting out a sigh, I tried not to seem overly excited. *But I was.* "Okay. If that's what you want."

She looked down at herself. "I need to get into something more presentable. Will you come upstairs for a bit and then we can come back down for breakfast together? You can dump all your stuff there, too."

I gathered my stuff as adrenaline pumped through me. "Let's go."

I followed Sarah back to her room and noticed she hadn't taken the mistletoe down.

"You kept it hanging."

"Yeah." She smiled as her cheeks reddened.

Before she had a chance to open the door, I pulled her toward me, taking her lips with mine. I just couldn't wait to taste her again. Sarah moaned into my mouth as she used the key card to open the door, our lips still locked, our tongues colliding.

"Maybe we could skip breakfast," she said into my mouth.

My heart thundered against my chest. I stopped and looked into her eyes. "I need you to clarify what you're insinuating because I'm too damn excited right now and could very well draw the wrong assumption."

"Do you want me, Kelly?" she whispered.

"Fuck, yes. I want you in every way." Pulling her close, I said, "And just to be clear, by that I mean more than just a vacation fling, Sarah. I want us to continue seeing each other when we get home...if that's what you want."

"It *is* what I want. And *also* to be clear, I'm not wearing anything under this."

I felt my dick stiffen. "Are you saying what I think you're saying?"

"I'm saying I want to get laid right now, if that's what you want, too."

My mouth curved into a huge smile as I nodded. "Sleighed."

Her eyes widened. "What?"

"Getting laid over Christmas time...'sleighed'."

She snorted. "That's probably the corniest thing you've said thus far, Fugger." She ran her hands through my hair. "It's a good thing you're irresistibly handsome...with special talents."

"You have no idea." I gestured toward my bag. "I've got two penis maracas in there I've got plans for—and a hungry tongue. It'll officially be next year by the time you want to leave this room." I lifted her up.

She wrapped her legs around me. "Well...Merry Fugging Christmas to me!"

LIGHTS OUT, LOVE

CHAPTER 1

Josie

"**W**hat in the hell are you doing?"

I was bent over, wrapping lights around the base of my mailbox, and the bark of a man's voice behind me made me jump. When I stood up, my head whacked against the mailbox above me.

"*Owww.*" I rubbed the top of my head and squinted at the man whose voice had startled me. My neighbor was parked in front of my house, sitting in his ridiculously large truck. "Jesus—don't sneak up on people like that. What the hell does it *look like* I'm doing?"

He glanced around my lawn. "It looks like someone vomited Christmas all over the place."

I scowled. God, this new neighbor was always so grumpy. It was too bad, because he was also pretty damn hot. He reminded me of that British actor from the Divergent movies...Theo something or other. But just because he had full lips, a chiseled jawline, and eyes the color of molten chocolate, didn't mean I'd put up with his insulting my pride-and-joy Christmas display.

My hands settled on my hips. "I'm just getting started. It takes me a full two weeks to get everything set up."

"You mean there's *more* than all this?"

"Of course there is."

He shook his head. "Those lights on your roof are already going to be shining in my window at night."

I almost laughed. He was worried about the two measly strings I'd put up this afternoon? This was *nothing* compared to what it would look like by December 1. I was pretty sure astronauts in space enjoyed the glow of my house during the holidays.

I shrugged. "Perhaps you should get those black-out shades people who work nights and sleep days use."

Mr. Grumpy frowned. Without a word, he nailed the gas and pulled into the driveway across from mine. I thought that was going to be the end of it, but after he got out of the car, he ambled back across the street.

"Please don't tell me all of this attracts attention and people come by at all hours of the night to see a bunch of lights and silly figurines moving on your lawn."

I pursed my lips. "Okay. I won't."

He narrowed his eyes. "You won't what?"

"I won't tell you that people come from all over to see my display, even though it's the truth."

Mr. Grumpy dragged a hand through his hair. "I bought this house because the neighborhood is quiet. Most of the homes around here are only used seasonally, and I travel most of the summer when it gets busy. I figured it would be empty in the winter."

He wasn't wrong. This area of the Hamptons was mostly second homes. The population in the summer grew to fifteen times what it was in the winter. Year-rounders like me weren't the norm.

"It is quiet for most of the winter," I said. Though I didn't bother to add that in just a few weeks, our little block would have a constant stream of cars passing by. People came from all the surrounding towns to see my decorations. He'd have to deal. After all, the money people donated when they came by went to charity.

Mr. Grumpy's eyes roamed my face. Apparently whatever he was looking for he didn't find, because he frowned and stomped back to his house without another word.

Sighing, I kneeled back down to finish setting up the mailbox lights and mumbled under my breath, "*So rude.*"

"Rude is being inconsiderate of the people around you!" my neighbor yelled as he walked up his driveway.

How the hell had he heard me?

I cupped my hands around my mouth and leaned toward his house as I yelled back, "Or saying someone's hard work looks like vomit!"

He responded with the loud slam of his front door.

What a jerk.

The following week, I went shopping with my friend Sarah for new decorations to add to my display. Sarah lived in Manhattan and mostly spent summers in the Hamptons, but all I'd had to do was *mention* shopping and she'd come out to visit me for the day.

Our mission complete, we'd started to unload the packed trunk of my car back home in my driveway. There had to be at least twenty bags of lights and decorations, plus the backseat had two gorgeous, six-foot-tall nutcrackers I'd snagged at an incredible pre-season sale. As I collected another handful of bags, Mr. Grumpy's big, obnoxious truck came down the street. I hadn't seen him since our lovely last encounter at my mailbox a few days ago. He shook his head as he rolled by and parked in his driveway.

My friend turned and caught a glimpse of the man behind the wheel. "*Ooooh...*" she cooed. "I forgot all about him. Hot Neighbor moved in during the spring, right? Why didn't we see him at all over the summer?"

I shrugged. "He bought the house in April, I think. But he wasn't around much until recently."

Sarah looked across the street and waved. "God, he's really gorgeous. Emily Vanderquint's husband mentioned him at your Labor Day party. He said he's some sort of author. Something about a summer book tour? Apparently he's very popular—that's probably why he wasn't around much."

"Yeah, well, he's also a jerk."

"Really?" She licked her lips. "I don't mind jerks. The bigger the chip on the shoulder, the hotter the sex. Are you...interested in him?"

I scoffed. "Definitely not. If he doesn't already hate me, he's going to in six days."

"So...you wouldn't mind if I went over and said hello, then?"

An unexpected pang of jealousy hit me, though that was ridiculous. I shrugged and closed the trunk. "Suit yourself. Have at it."

Sarah smiled, smoothed her hair, and gave a little tug to the hem of her sweater, which caused the V-neck to showcase more cleavage.

"Leave the big nutcrackers in the backseat," she said. "I'm going to ask him for help lifting them out."

"Uhhh... That's probably not a good idea. The man loathes my Christmas display."

But Sarah was already walking across the street. She raised a hand and called out as he walked to his front door. "Yoo-hoo! Mr. Neighbor Man!"

I rolled my eyes and headed to the garage to store the packages from my trunk. A few minutes later, Sarah came back with Mr. Grumpy in tow.

"Cole here is going to help us lift out those heavy nut-crackers."

I smirked at him. "Cole? Is that your real name or what old Saint Nick leaves in your stocking because you're such a scrooge?"

Mr. Grumpy tried to keep a stoic face, but I caught the little twitch at the corner of his mouth. Sarah opened the back door of my car, and he peered inside.

"Gee, a nutcracker for the woman who likes to bust my balls. How appropriate."

"Good one." I laughed. "Your wittiness doesn't make up for your grumpiness, though."

Sarah interrupted, "I, uh, actually have to run—late for an appointment. Have fun!"

She disappeared, getting into her car before I could even give her a dirty look. She'd intentionally left me alone with this curmudgeon guy.

He watched her drive away, then turned to me. "So why exactly am I contributing to this holiday vomit again?"

I tilted my head. "Because deep down you have a soul, *Cole*?"

"Nope, that can't be it. I gave up my soul for Lent last year and never got it back." He winked, flashing a mischievous smile that made me tingle a bit.

Cole the Asshole was downright hotter than hell.

"Well, I appreciate you letting me borrow your muscles in any case," I said.

He looked around at the decorations and lights I'd put up thus far. "Seriously, why do you bother with all this? It's a lot of work. Why not just go visit lights somewhere else?"

"If everyone thought that way, there would be nothing in life to enjoy. Sometimes you have to be the change you want to see in the world." I tried to disregard the emotions bubbling up, because deep down, I knew that wasn't my only motivation. "Anyway...I have my reasons."

Cole raised a brow. "You get off on the attention?"

"If attention means making other people happy, then yes, I get off on it." I squinted. "And by the way, given that you've chosen not to participate in our block's line of lights, don't be surprised if you see kids crying when they pass your house because it's such a disappointment. You're going to stick out like a sore thumb, being the only dark house."

"There's only five houses on our little block, and I haven't seen a light on in two of them in weeks."

I pointed to each home as I spoke. "The Martins' son will be here this weekend to put up their decorations. They winter in Florida, but their son still comes and sets up a simple display that works on a timer. The Ackermans hire a company to set up theirs, and old Mrs. Becker comes out and puts up her own lights even though she's nearly eighty. It's for charity, and it looks nice when the whole block is lit up around my display. *You're* the only scrooge."

"I'll live with that guilt, but thanks for the warning." He bent to reach into my backseat. "Anyway, let me get these out for you." I watched as my neighbor slowly and carefully lifted the first heavy soldier out of the car. "Where do you want him?"

I pointed. "On the left side of my front door, please. The other can go right across on the opposite side." I snorted. 'They're going to be standing guard."

"Awesome," he said. He deposited the soldier and returned to the car. "And to think I just installed a home security system. Had I known these things were going to be protecting the neighborhood, I wouldn't have bothered."

After he placed the second soldier in its rightful spot, I said, "Well, thank you for the help."

He rolled his eyes. "Maybe Santa Claus will be nice to me this year."

For some reason, I felt like I should offer him something to say thanks. "Would you...like to come in for a glass of wine?" *What am I doing?*

He scratched his chin, looking down at his shoes. "Actually, I can't. I have a virtual meeting for work in a few minutes."

"Or it could be that you don't want to fraternize with the overly jolly neighbor." I chuckled, feeling dumb for asking him to come over. "What exactly do you hate so much about Christmas lights anyway?"

"Well, for one, it invites unnecessary attention. There's a lot to be said for peace on the home front. I want to be able to walk around in my underwear without having to worry about someone peering in my window."

"Christmas has to stop because you don't want to wear pants?"

"Well, I didn't know what I was signing up for when I moved to Santa's Village."

That made me crack up. "Fair enough. Anyway, thank you for the help."

"No problem." He nodded and headed back across the street.

I watched as he walked away, enjoying the view of his mighty fine backside, and imagined him prancing around in his underwear to the tune of "Jingle Bell Rock" coming from my front lawn.

CHAPTER 2

Cole

All men manscape, right?

It was time for my once-a-month trimming. So I stripped off my clothes and stood in front of the bathroom mirror, taking some time to appreciate the results of the hard work I'd been putting in at the gym.

As I turned on the razor, I thought about my crazy neighbor Josie. I might've given her shit, but she was pretty damn cute. Too bad she reminded me of someone I wanted to forget, and that made me uneasy around her.

Josie. Trimming her tree across the street, while I was over here trimming the hedges around my cock.

Laughing inwardly, I'd just started to shave the first section when everything went black. The lights in the bathroom had gone out.

"What the fuck?"

I was pretty sure I'd shaved over something I hadn't intended to. I turned off the razor and exited the bathroom, only to find that the lights in the entire rest of the house were out, too.

I looked out the window. The other houses on the street were also dark. Then it hit me: *Josie*. Today was the first evening of her lights display. It had nearly blinded me on my way back from having a drink with some friends. This was the first night of her holiday shenanigans, and suddenly all the power went out? There was no way those two things had nothing to do with each other.

I couldn't see shit, but I made my way to my closet and grabbed what felt like a pair of jeans. I huffed and pulled them on before finding a shirt to throw over my head.

I carefully ventured downstairs and grabbed a flashlight from under the kitchen sink. Then I walked across the street to Josie's. There didn't seem to be anyone home at the other neighbors' houses. They now had decorations out, but I hadn't noticed their lights on earlier tonight. Clearly Josie had blown the entire street.

She was already standing in front of her house when I got there, as if she'd been expecting me.

Her hands were on her hips. "So...your wish came true," she said. "Now not only are my lights out, but the whole street's gone dark. Happy?"

She's got to be kidding. She's putting this on me? I shook my head. "Yeah. I'm thrilled. I love writing in the dark when I'm on deadline. I especially love when my laptop isn't charged, and I have no way of even getting to my manuscript." I shook my head. "Is this a common occurrence when you drain the neighborhood of power?"

"Don't put this on me. It's not my fault the lights went out. I blame your bad juju more than me using a little extra power."

I scoffed. "A *little* extra power? That's like saying the Kardashians are *a little* overexposed." The woman had a full ice rink set up in her driveway with a half-dozen life-

size skaters milling around to damn Christmas music—
and that wasn't a fraction of the shit she had going on.

"Maybe it was *you* who blew the power," she coun-
tered. "I see you messing with saws and stuff in the garage
sometimes. What power tool were *you* tinkering with today when the power blew?"

That almost made me laugh. I'd been messing with a
power tool alright... I cleared my throat. "How long does
this usually last?"

"I don't know." She huffed. "The power has never gone
out before."

Great. Just freaking great. "Well, did you at least
call?"

"No...*did you?*"

I sighed and raked a hand through my hair. "Do you
have some candles? I'm not exactly prepared for a black-
out."

Josie nodded. "I do. But can you come in the house
with that flashlight so I can dig them out? I had to use the
batteries from my flashlight for something on my display."

I mumbled, "Of course you did."

The inside of Josie's house smelled like a bakery. I
shined the light into the kitchen. "Were you making cookies or something?"

"Chocolate chip and pumpkin oatmeal raisin. You
want one?"

Considering I was salivating at the smell, and my plans
had been to use electricity to microwave a frozen dinner
later, it didn't seem wise to pass up the offer. "Sure."

"Can you point that flashlight at the table, please? It's
to your right."

I moved the light that direction, and my eyes went
wide. "How many freaking cookies did you make?" There

had to be at least a dozen trays lined up on her table, each one with a heaping mound of cookies wrapped in cellophane.

She peeled back the wrapping on one of the trays and slipped out two cookies. Passing them to me, she said, "I made eighteen dozen. Last year I made fifteen on the first night, and I ran out an hour before the end of the evening."

"Jesus, I figured you got traffic, but not those kind of numbers. I didn't think there were a hundred-and-eighty people left in this part of Westhampton Beach."

She smiled. "I teach third grade in East Hampton. A lot of my students come—some are in college now and still come back every year."

I bit into one of the cookies. "Damn. These are good. I guess if I had a teacher who looked like you and made shit that tasted like this, I'd probably still be coming back at my age."

Even with only the light from the flashlight, I could see Josie blush. That surprised me; she had to be used to compliments with the way she looked.

"Umm...my candles should be in the top drawer of the sideboard in the dining room," she said. "Follow me with your flashlight."

She pulled a bunch of candles from a drawer, and then walked to the mantel over the fireplace and grabbed a lighter. After lighting a few candles around the room, she handed me two unlit ones.

"Here you go. These are from Thanksgiving, so they might smell like pumpkin or spices."

I nodded. "Thanks."

The flicker of the candle she held in her hand caught the blue of her eyes, and *damn*, her eyes were gorgeous. I forced my gaze elsewhere and nodded toward the door.

"I'll, uh, head back over to my place and give the power company a call."

"Okay. Thanks. I'll call and report the power outage, too."

Three hours later, I called the electric company a second time to see if they had an ETA on restoring service, but they still had no clue. I really needed to get some work done. My truck had an outlet, so I figured I'd go sit in the car to charge my laptop enough to see where I'd left off in my manuscript. At least then I could write using paper and pen tonight. But when I raised the garage door so I wouldn't suffocate myself with exhaust fumes, I looked across the street and saw two rooms lit up over at Josie's house.

What the fuck? They restored her power and not mine?

How long had she had electricity?

Rather than start the truck, I marched across the street and knocked on Josie's door.

"When did you get your power back?"

"Oh..." she said. "I didn't. I have a gas generator. I went to the gas station a little while ago."

I frowned and lifted the laptop in my hand. "Do you mind if I charge this?"

"No, of course not." She stepped aside for me to enter and pointed to a power strip on the floor in the living room. "Go right ahead. Help yourself."

After I plugged in and made sure my laptop was charging, I glanced around to see what her house looked like in the light. "I'll be back in, like, an hour to pick it up, if that's okay?"

"Sure."

On my way to the front door, Josie called after me.

"Cole?"

I stopped. "Yeah?"

"Are you hungry? I just put in a tray of homemade manicotti."

While I debated the pros of a good meal with the cons of spending time with a woman who reminded me of Jessica, my stomach growled. *Loudly.*

Josie laughed. "I'll take that as a yes."

"Uhhh..." I shrugged. "Sure, why not?"

Twenty minutes later, we were sitting at the dining room table. Since Josie's living room didn't have a lamp to plug into a power strip, we ate our meal by candlelight.

The room was so quiet. I watched as she refilled her wine glass. Mid-pour, she looked up and caught my eyes on her.

"What?" she said.

I shook my head. "Nothing."

"Well, you're staring at me, so it's not nothing. Tell me what you were just thinking."

Since *what your lips taste like* probably wasn't a good answer, I said something else I had wondered about. "What got you started with the Christmas over-decorating?"

She smiled sadly. "William. William got me started. He was a student of mine. I had him in class nine years ago, in my second year of teaching. He had spina bifida and was confined to a wheelchair, but you'd never know it from his attitude. He was the happiest child I've ever met—and he *loved* Christmas. He used to decorate his wheelchair with lights and ornaments two months before the holiday. Because of his spinal-cord issues, he'd had quite a few back surgeries. He was preparing for his sixth one, which was scheduled for after our school year ended.

It was supposed to give him a chance to walk with a walker for the first time ever. The last thing he said to me before summer break was that everything was going to be okay because he had asked Santa for sea legs in December." Josie shook her head and wiped a tear from her eye. "An unexpected blood clot broke apart during his surgery. It went to his heart. He died on the table."

"Jesus. I'm sorry."

She wiped another tear. "It's okay. You would think after almost ten years, I'd be able to talk about it without crying. But apparently not."

"You have every reason to be upset. There's no time-line for healing from something like that."

Josie forced a smile. "Thank you. Anyway...I wanted to do something to honor William. So the next year I did a big Christmas display and put out a collection box for donations to the Spina Bifida Association. Some of the parents heard about it and came and made donations. One thing led to another, and each year I made the display bigger and more kids came. We've collected more than fif-ty-thousand dollars over the last nine holiday seasons."

"Wow. That's awesome."

"Yeah. William would be thrilled about the display, so it makes me happy to do it each year."

And here I was avoiding this woman because she re-minded me of Jessica. This woman was nothing like my ex. She was kind and caring, and damn, she could cook.

I forked another bite of the manicotti and stopped with it halfway to my mouth. "This is delicious, by the way. Best meal I've had in...I don't know how long."

"Thank you. Have more. I have a bad habit of cooking for four even though it's just little old me."

Josie really seemed like the whole package, so how come it was just *little old her*? "Why is that?"

"Why do I cook for four?"

"No, why isn't there anyone in your life to cook for?"

"Oh..." She shrugged. "I don't know. I date once in a while. Had a boyfriend for a while, but we broke up last year. So I guess...I just haven't met the right person."

I nodded.

Josie sipped her wine. "Are you sure you don't want some? This merlot is delicious."

I'd declined earlier since I had to work tonight. But when she offered a second time, I couldn't resist. "Sure, why not?"

She poured me a glass and looked at me over the brim of hers. "And you—what's your story?" She motioned to my empty plate. "I take it from the way you just scarfed down that food that you don't have a woman in your life cooking for you?"

I shook my head. "No woman in my life anymore. But even when the last one was still around, I didn't get a home-cooked meal. My ex, Jessica, burned water."

Josie laughed. "I'm sure she wasn't that bad."

"She tried to make me a birthday cake one year. She set the oven on fire. The fire department trashed my kitchen putting it out."

Josie chuckled, probably assuming I was exaggerating. Sadly, I wasn't.

I gazed across the table at her, taking in her smile. The candlelight cast a glow on her face that created an angelic aura. She really was beautiful, and at the moment, while her guard was down, she looked vulnerable. It made me want to be honest with her.

"I apologize for being so harsh with you about your Christmas display."

"It's okay. I get how the traffic can be annoying, especially to someone who works from home and counts on quiet."

I looked down at my plate for a moment. "My being an asshole actually had nothing to do with your Christmas display, if I'm being truthful."

She gave me a look. "No?"

I shook my head. "You sort of remind me of someone, and that might've made me a little extra grumpy toward you."

Josie's forehead wrinkled. "I remind you of someone?"

I nodded. "My ex had long, dark hair and light skin like you. She was thin and...well, curvy like you. She also drove the same red Audi you do and loved the holidays—although she loved Christmas because it meant shopping and receiving gifts. Not for the right reasons, like you do."

"So you were a jerk to me because I resembled your ex-girlfriend?"

"Now you think I'm an even bigger asshole, right?"

She laughed. "I never really thought you were an asshole. There's usually a reason when someone is so negative. It's not about their feelings toward others; it's a reflection of themselves—what they feel about themselves specifically, their own fears and hang-ups."

I tilted my head. "Ah. You're very analytical. I should interview you for one of my articles."

Her eyes sparkled. "What is it that you write?"

I wiped my mouth. "I'm a researcher specializing in the connection between neuroscience, psychology, and epigenetics. I write a series of articles about the mind-body connection, how changing your mindset can change your health and your life as a whole."

Her mouth dropped. "My grumpy-pants neighbor is a self-help guru? I would've never guessed that."

"Well, there are lots of ironies in life, right?"

"I've often wondered what you wrote, like maybe you were a Nicholas Sparks-type author writing under a secret pen name. That always made me laugh because romance seems like the antithesis of you."

I chuckled. "Because I've been so warm and fuzzy?"

She shook her head. "Right."

"Well, a lot of people think the information I put out is a crock of shit. But I've seen some amazing things happen when people are able to rewire their brains." I sighed. "Admittedly, though, sometimes I don't practice what I preach. I still get into the habit of not taking care of myself, dwelling on the past, or allowing anger and stress into my life on a daily basis, even though I know there are steps I can take to control those things."

She nodded. "So, how does one do that exactly— change their brain?"

"There's not a simple answer to that question. But the gist is a combination of physical and mental work. For example, what you put into your body is important..."

I paused at the unexpected and definitely inappropriate visual my words elicited.

"You mean like food?" she asked.

Yes. Like food—not my penis.

"Exactly. But not only that—how you spend your time and the people you spend your time with also affect your life more than you know. Removing yourself from stressful situations is key, as is finding a way to get out of your head, even if for just ten minutes a day through meditation. Stress is killer. It literally causes disease." I moved some of the remaining food around on my plate, warning myself not to go off on a tangent. "Anyway...if you want to know more, I have dozens of articles on my website."

She leaned in. "I'm intrigued. Can you show me where to find them?"

I picked up my phone and typed in the address before handing it to her.

Josie scrolled through. "Wow. You've written so many articles! How do you come up with the topics? And why aren't there photos of you anywhere on here?"

"The company I work for prefers to keep it more about the information and not the source. I have no desire to become famous anyway."

She looked up from the phone. "Such a shame and a marketing fail on their part, because you're really hand-some." Her cheeks turned red.

She's fucking adorable. I cleared my throat, unsure how to handle the compliment. "Thank you."

Our eyes locked for a moment before Josie handed me back the phone.

"So, what's next? What topic are you working on now?"

I sighed. "Actually, I've been stuck lately. I'm on a deadline, and I'm struggling with where to take my latest article. Not sure what to focus on."

She moved her chair back and stood up. "Well, don't let me keep you from working. Your laptop has to be fully charged by now."

Oddly, I didn't exactly want to get up. I'd enjoyed talking to her, even if I'd opened up a bit too much.

"Yeah..." I sighed. "At this rate, I'll be up all night writ-ing."

"What if you lose your charge again?"

"I guess I'll just be screwed."

She bit her lip. "Why don't you work here for a while? Just keep it plugged in, and then when you're ready to head back to your place, you'll still have all the juice left."

Her offer was more than gracious, considering what a dick I'd been to her. "Are you sure?"

"Yeah. I'm positive."

"Thank you. I think I'll take you up on that."

After we cleaned up our plates, I settled into a spot in Josie's couch next to the power strip.

Soon after, I could hear her shower running upstairs, and my mind went wild imagining what she looked like naked under that water.

After a few minutes of enjoying that mental imagery, something miraculous happened as I stared at the empty page on my computer. I started to type. Deep down, I knew why my writer's block had gone away. This place, as much as I'd knocked Josie in the past, was a warm and welcoming environment that relaxed me. And because I was able to calm my mind, ideas started to move freely within it. The words flowed as I began to write about my experience tonight. The title of the piece was: *Change Your Environment, Change Your Productivity*.

I got more than a thousand words down in a matter of twenty minutes.

When I paused, I took in a deep whiff of the scented candles mixed with the lingering smell of cookies in the air. Was it really this place? Or was it *her*—knowing she was right upstairs and that for the first time in a long time, I wasn't alone. My chest constricted, and my body tightened defensively.

Don't get too comfortable, Cole.

Footsteps registered behind me, and then Josie appeared, wearing a long shirt that had snowflakes all over it. It went down almost to her knees, but most notably, it was thin enough to display the outline of her ample breasts much more clearly than her shirt had earlier. God, she was beautiful. I didn't want to like her. *But I did.*

Josie moved a piece of her dark hair behind her ear. "I, uh, wanted to say goodnight. Stay as long as you like." She handed me a key. "Just lock the door from the outside with this. It's a spare. You can give it back to me tomorrow."

"Thank you. I can't tell you how much I appreciate this."

She walked over to the counter before returning with a plate of cookies.

"Just in case you need some middle-of-the-night fuel."

Her eyes glimmered in the candlelight. As good as the cookies smelled, there was nothing I wanted more than a taste of *her*. I shook my head. I needed to get my mind out of this fantasyland and focus. No way could I let myself fall for someone who looked so much like Jessica. I'd never be able to rid myself of the association, and it would end badly. It had to—I'd never allow myself to get hurt like that again. And that meant my defense mechanisms would end up hurting Josie. She didn't deserve that.

After she went upstairs, my writing streak continued. In fact, I was so into my writing that at some point, my body completely shut down.

I didn't realize it until Josie tapped me on my shoulder the next morning.

CHAPTER 3

Josie

"Good morning, sleepyhead." I smiled. It had been a while since a man had slept over. "I'm sorry to wake you. I have to go out to East Hampton to put my grades in the computer for report cards since the Wi-Fi isn't working yet. I didn't want you to wake up and the house be empty."

Cole sat up and dragged a hand through his hair. "Shit. What time is it? I must've fallen asleep on the couch while I was working last night. Sorry about that."

"No problem. And it's almost nine. You were really out cold. I came downstairs and made coffee, took a shower, and even unloaded the dishwasher. You didn't move a muscle."

I shook my head. "Nine o'clock? Wow. I can't remember the last time I slept past six."

"How late did you work last night?"

"I'm not sure. But I got a lot done."

"I'm glad. Would you like a cup of coffee?"

Cole stood. He lifted his hands over his head to stretch, and his sweater rode up, revealing some pretty impressive abs and a sexy line of hair that ran from his navel down into his pants. *Damn*, he wasn't just a pretty face; he had a body to match. I thought he might've caught me ogling him, so I pretended I'd been looking down at my shoe and quickly knelt to tie my sneaker, even though it wasn't untied.

"No, I'm good," he said. "I don't want to trouble you. I've already put you out enough. I'll make a pot when I get home."

"Umm...no, you won't. We still don't have any power."

"Shit...right." He looked around. "I forgot since it's light out now, and you have a generator. I'll run out and grab some at Dunkin' Donuts. I don't want to make you late."

I waved him off. "It's fine. I can show up anytime today to enter my grades. I'm not in a rush."

"Alright. Well, if you have it made, I'll take a cup, please."

In the kitchen, I poured two mugs of coffee. I added a little half and half to mine and held up the carton to Cole. "Do you take cream or sugar?"

"No. Just black, please."

I passed him his coffee. "You know, I could have guessed that. You seem like a black coffee kind of guy."

"Oh yeah?" He leaned his hip against the kitchen counter and sipped. "What exactly are the characteristics of a black coffee kind of guy?"

I shrugged. "I don't know... I guess they're sort of... like you."

He chuckled. "So maybe like a neighbor who backs over those flower beds you have at the end of the driveway and doesn't say anything?"

"Actually, you'd probably say something. You'd tell me it was my fault."

Cole hung his head and laughed. "I can see I made a really good impression on you."

I waved him off. "Eh, it's okay. Some of the best men I know come across as stoic and grumpy, but deep down they have a heart of gold. My dad and brother are that way, so I don't give up easily on people. I keep looking until I find something redeeming."

Cole smiled. "Thank you. I appreciate that."

"By the way," I said. "I finally got through to the electric company this morning. There's a twenty-block power outage. There was a fire in the main transformer or something like that—so it wasn't my fault after all. But they said it could be two or three days before we get full power restored."

Cole sighed. "Great. I guess I'll pick up a generator today." He finished drinking his coffee and rinsed his mug in the sink. "Thank you again for letting me use your electricity last night. And again, I apologize for overstaying my welcome."

I set my coffee mug in the sink. "Actually, it works out well that you stayed. Now when I call my mother this weekend and she asks how things are going on the *man front*, I can tell her I had a man stay over the other night, and I won't be lying."

Cole's eyes did a quick sweep over my body, and he flashed a sexy grin. "You better tell her I was good."

"Oh, no worries. You were fantastic."

He nodded with a smile. "Thank you. I aim to please."

For some reason—the same way I'd known he would take his coffee black—I was certain Cole was indeed a man who would aim to please in bed. As I walked him to the door, I stole a glance at his firm ass. His jeans hugged him nicely, and I imagined his naked derrière matched his muscular abs.

He turned around unexpectedly, and my eyes jumped to meet his.

"Well, if you can't find a generator for some reason," I said, "you're welcome to come back and work here again tonight or charge your laptop or whatever you need." I wrote down my phone number on a piece of paper. "Just text me first so I know you're coming over."

Cole smiled as he took the number. "Thanks, Josie. Have a good day."

"You, too."

After work, I stopped and ran some errands. So when I pulled into my driveway, it was already starting to get dark. I took two bags of groceries out of the trunk of my car and looked over at my neighbor's house. There weren't any lights on, but there was a ladder set up out front. And were those *Christmas lights* strung over the windows? Why yes, yes, they were. My sexy scrooge neighbor was hanging holiday decorations?

I set the bags in my arms back down in the trunk and strolled across the street. Cole walked out his front door just as I reached the top of his driveway.

"Scrooge hung up Christmas lights?" I asked. "Am I seeing things?"

He smiled. "I figured it was the least I could do since you let me borrow your generator and crash on your couch.

I thought you might like the entire block lit up better than a bottle of wine or something to say thank you."

"I do! I love that you did all that for me."

"Good." Cole held up one finger. "Hang on a sec." He disappeared into his house and came back out carrying a brown paper bag. Extending it to me, he said, "I also bought you wine, in case the lights weren't enough."

I felt warmth in my belly, even though it was cold outside. "Thank you. That was very thoughtful."

"No problem. But confession...I might also have bought it because I need to butter you up. The store was sold out of generators. My laptop is almost out of juice again. If you don't mind, it would be great if I could plug in and charge it later."

"Oh, sure. No problem." I nodded toward the house. "Do you like tortellini alfredo? That's what I'm making for dinner. We could share this bottle and eat while your laptop charges. Think of how excited my mom will be if I tell her a man slept over *and* he came for dinner the very next night?"

Cole smiled. "Well, when you put it like that... I wouldn't want to disappoint Mom."

"Great. I'll let you finish putting up your beautiful lights, and I'll get started cooking. Come over around seven?"

"I'll be there."

I had ninety minutes before Cole would arrive. After putting all of my groceries away, I was just about to start preparing dinner when the lights in my dining room suddenly turned on. Then I heard random beeping throughout the house—the sound of various electronics coming back to life.

Oh my God! The power is back!

As lucky as I was to have the generator, there was nothing like fully functioning power. Relief washed over me. I'd been truly worried they'd never get things fixed, and that Christmas—which was only a week away—was going to be ruined.

Within minutes, my phone rang. It was Cole.

I picked up. "Hey! Did you get your power back?"

"Yup. Wasn't expecting that—way sooner than they estimated. Christmas came early, I guess."

I exhaled. "What a relief. I was just about to start dinner when the lights came on."

There was a pause. Then he said, "You haven't started cooking yet?"

"No."

"Good. Because I, uh, probably won't be coming by. I appreciate the offer, but I should go to the store instead—reload my fridge, take care of some things around here now that the power is back."

Disappointment filled me. "Oh...okay. Are you sure you don't just want to eat and run? I'm cooking anyway."

There was a moment of silence. Then he said, "I probably shouldn't."

I felt a little sad—and stupid. I thought Cole and I had hit it off pretty well. Maybe it was delusional to think there was something there. He apparently didn't want to hang out with me. He'd just been using me for electricity.

"Okay, well, I hope you get a lot done," I said in a short tone.

"Thank you. And thanks again for being so awesome through all this."

Before I hung up, I felt compelled to ask him a question. "Cole?"

"Yeah?"

"I know Christmas isn't your favorite holiday, so I was wondering... Which Christmas song is your least favorite?"

"*Least* favorite?"

"Yes. Least."

"Hmm..." He laughed. "Probably 'All I Want For Christmas is You.' It's overplayed."

"Ah. I actually love that one. But okay. Fair answer based on the overplayed part."

"Why did you want to know my least favorite and not my favorite?"

"I found that to be the more interesting question."

"I do have a favorite," he said. "Wanna know what it is?"

"What?"

"It's 'Grandma Got Run Over By a Reindeer.'"

I rolled my eyes. "Why does that not surprise me?"

CHAPTER 4

Cole

I blinked my eyes open after waking from a nightmare. I hadn't even remembered nodding off. Once again, writer's block had bitten me in the ass, and I'd fallen asleep with my computer on my lap in the middle of the damn afternoon. That wasn't a surprise, considering I'd been up almost the entire night before.

It had been a few days since power was restored, but my life felt no brighter. I'd chickened out about going over to Josie's the other night because my feelings for her scare me. When the power came back, I suddenly had an out, so I took it.

And now, here I was with drool on my face after waking up from a dream where the words on my screen turned into snakes that crawled out of the computer to strangle me. All this while the *Happy Days* theme song played in the background. If that wasn't fucked up, I didn't know what was.

I looked at the clock. It was 7PM.

Outside, Josie's spectacular lights display was in full swing. It was just a few days before Christmas now, and people were gathered across the street, taking it all in.

Josie held some kind of tray. It looked like she was passing out hot apple cider or eggnog. Maybe cocoa. My stomach felt tight. I longed to be over there. Not necessarily with all of those people—but with her. *Only with her.* I just hadn't been willing to explore the possibility that she was different from my lying, cheating ex. And why? She'd given me no reason to believe she was anything like Jessica. But fear was a bitch. *A bigger bitch than Jessica.* And I'd let fear rule my decisions. That went against everything I'd ever preached about when it came to positive thinking. But in order to get past nagging fears, you have to accept uncertainty. That's the basis for most tactics to reduce worry; yet I'd been unable to do it.

The crowd of people began to line up in front of Josie's house. I soon realized they were singing. It was a choir of some kind. And it wasn't just any song they were belting out. Cold air billowed into my house as I opened the window to better hear the sound of freaking "All I Want For Christmas is You."

Is she kidding me?

Nice, Josie. Nice.

I burst into laughter.

It was no coincidence. That had to have been meant for me. Maybe it wasn't. Either way, it was funny.

After a couple of minutes, I shut the window and attempted to get work done with the muffled sounds of Christmas chaos outside.

At least the lame lights I'd put up out front were better than the total darkness I'd originally planned. Now instead of Scrooge, I was just the lonely writer across the street, afraid to go all the way at anything in life, a fear accurately reflected through my measly, half-assed holiday display.

After several minutes of being unable to focus, I shut my laptop, deciding to go downstairs and make myself something to eat.

Before I opened the fridge, I grabbed the stack of mail sitting on the counter and began to sift through it. Among the bills were a couple of Christmas cards. I opened the first one to find it was from my brother—a shot of my two-year-old nephew, Benjamin, dressed as an elf. It made my cold heart happy for a couple of seconds before I tossed it aside to open the next envelope.

Inside was a small card and a photo of someone I didn't recognize: a boy in a wheelchair. Next to him was a beautiful brunette I *did* recognize: Josie. I realized this card wasn't meant for me. It had been mistakenly delivered here.

But I'd already opened it, and I remembered the story she'd told me about her former student, William—her inspiration for the Christmas display. So I read the message inside.

Dear Josie,

We know this Christmas will be the best one yet. But we say that every year when it comes to your extravaganza of lights. We thought you'd enjoy this old photo we found of you and our guy. Can you believe William would have been graduating high school this year? Thank you for helping his memory to live on. We will see you soon.

Love,
The Testinos

I stared at the photo of the smiling boy, who seemed so filled with joy and hope. He hadn't had it easy. He'd had to accept a lot of uncertainty every day of his life. But he'd still managed to find happiness. He wasn't supposed to die on that operating table. I shook my head, feeling myself tear up. I didn't even know the kid. I couldn't imagine how Josie felt. *Life is so damn fleeting.* And here I was, obsessing over my past—a past that held no significance over my present. I was here in this lonely house when I really wanted to be across the street. Not because of the lights, but because of the single ray of light responsible for it all.

I spoke to the photo in my hand. "William, thank you for the reminder that I've been a complete and utter idiot. Pretty sure this card was meant for me after all."

The following day, I went shopping.

"Excuse me, are there any other decorations in the back?"

The sales clerk shook her head. "Just what you see here. We put the Christmas stuff out before Halloween these days, so we're pretty much sold out by the first week in December."

This was the third store I'd gone to. The only crap left was...well, crap. Nothing more than a bunch of lights and some of those dumb blow-ups—and even those were picked over. My choices were a six-foot-tall inflatable menorah, a polar bear hugging an ornament, or palm trees.

I sighed. "Thanks."

After an hour and a half of going store to store, I started to think my brilliant idea might be over before it even began. But on my way out, I walked by the toy department. As I passed, I noticed a life-size figure down one of the aisles. Backing up a few steps, I lifted my chin to the kid stocking the shelf next to the display.

"You got any more of those?"

"Chewbacca?" His brow wrinkled. "They're right here."

"No, I meant any other big characters like that?"

"Oh, yeah. Next aisle over. I think there's, like, eight different ones or something. It's part of an anniversary of one of the movies."

"Can they go outside?"

The kid looked at the giant action figure next to him and shrugged. "I guess so. They don't have electronics or anything. That's probably why they didn't sell. They just kind of sit there."

The wheels in my head started to turn. "Is there a Yoda?"

"Yeah, but he's not as big."

Well, of course not. Chewbacca isn't the same size as Yoda. "Do you think he'd fit in a bassinet?"

"Who?"

"Yoda."

"Oh. What's a bassinet?"

Seriously? "It's like a small crib. Sort of like the manger they put baby Jesus in."

The kid shrugged. "Check aisle nine."

A half hour later, I had three carts at the checkout line. The silver-haired woman ringing me up smiled. "Your kids are *Star Wars* fans, huh?"

"Uhh...yeah."

"I bet these put a big smile on someone's face."

I held out my credit card and grinned. "That's what I'm hoping for."

After I finished at Target, I stopped at the local farm supply store a few miles away.

"Can I help you with something?" the guy behind the register said.

"Yeah, I need a some hay."

"We keep the hay around back. There's a fenced area with a green awning. You pay here and pull your car around the rear of the building. Give your receipt to the kid at the gate. How many bales do you need?"

"I think one should do it."

The guy nodded and punched some keys on his register. "Anything else I can get you today?"

"No, I think I'm good." I glanced around the store and saw one of those plastic owls that people use to scare away birds. "Actually..." I nodded toward the owl. "Would you happen to have any other plastic animals?"

"I think we have a doe and fawn set somewhere around here. People put 'em out more as a decoration than a deterrent though."

"Can I see them?"

He walked out from behind the counter and pointed toward the back of the store. "Follow me."

As I trailed behind the guy, I started to get a vision of what my creation was going to look like on the front lawn. Either this was going to be funny as hell, or Josie was going to think I was nuts.

"Here we go." The clerk pointed to two brown plastic deer with white Bambi spots. One was lying down and the other standing. "Is this the type of thing you're looking for?"

"This is *exactly* what I need. Any chance you also have one of those things a shepherd holds in his hand."

The guy's bushy eyebrows drew together, almost forming a straight line. "You mean a crook?"

"Yeah, I think that's what it's called."

He shook his head. "Sorry. We don't get a lot of sheep around here. But we've got a ketch-all."

"What's that?"

"It's a pole used to catch animals, but the top has a big loop around it, instead of a hook like a shepherd's crook."

I shrugged. "Okay, I'll take one of those instead. And maybe a pitchfork or two."

The guy helped me gather the rest of my purchases. As he finished ringing me up, he said, "Whatcha trying to catch?"

I smiled. "A woman."

The look on the guy's face was absolutely priceless. Though it was probably best to get the hell out of there before he called the cops on me.

Back at home, I didn't see Josie's car in the driveway. So I went to work, setting up my display. The entire thing took me more than four hours to put together—I cut wood from the garage and assembled something resembling the arch of a stable and decorated it with white lights. Half-a-dozen *Star Wars* characters huddled around the hay-filled bassinet manger, where baby Yoda laid peacefully. I added a few blow-up palm trees with lights, and the pair of deer completed the nutty scene. It had started to get dark by the time I finished everything. Yet my neighbor still wasn't home. I knew from the last few nights that her display went on promptly at seven—so it shouldn't be long now before she pulled up.

CHAPTER 5

Josie

Today had been the worst. Between a tense parent-teacher conference and the principal holding an unexpected staff meeting after school, I was mentally exhausted. Thankfully, it was the last day before Christmas break.

I vowed to pick myself up and get ready for tonight's display. I'd planned to make cookies and pass out cocoa and needed to be able to do it with a smile on my face. But maybe I'd light everything up a little later than usual and take a hot bath first to decompress.

As I pulled onto my street, the craziest sight met my eyes. While my house was dark, since I hadn't turned on the lights yet, Cole's was lit up much more brightly than ever before. Well, if this wasn't an ironic visual.

And it wasn't just the lights.

Oh my God. What am I looking at?

I abruptly parked on the street, not even bothering to pull into my driveway.

As soon as I exited the car, I noticed the music. Blasting from a speaker was the theme to...*Star Wars*? Within a few seconds, I realized why he'd chosen that. Cole had set up a nativity scene featuring life-size *Stars Wars* figures. A rifle-wielding Han Solo stood alone near a cradle. I peeked in and found Yoda inside. *Baby Yoda Jesus.* Chewbacca, Darth Vader, and Jabba the Hutt were lined up, I guessed as the three wise men. R2-D2 and C-3PO were chilling together on the other side of the lawn as shepherds. And there were palm trees and deer—oh my! He'd put up so many more lights, too.

What in the world?

When the door opened and Cole came outside, I nearly lost it.

"What the heck happened to you?" I asked. "Have you lost your mind?" My eyes traveled from top to bottom over his body. Cole wore a wig with buns on each side and a long white...dress.

"Someone had to be Princess Leia." He shrugged. "You can't have a *Star Wars* scene without her. They didn't have her at Target, so I found a costume store about thirty miles away. Figured I'd take one for the team."

I looked around. "And what a team it is..."

"By the way, you hit the nail on the head. I did finally lose my mind—my toxic mind. It needed to go." He held his arms up. "Because this is what it's all about, isn't it?"

"Sure. What's life without a *Star Wars* nativity?" I shook my head. "What's gotten into you?"

"I'll show you." Cole disappeared into the house for a moment. Then he handed me a card. I immediately recognized it as a Christmas card from William's family.

"I got this accidentally," he said. "I took one look at William's face and suddenly, I understood on a deeper level why you do what you do every year. His spirit made me reflect on myself. I realized that by living in fear, I wasn't living at all. And then I also decided, if you can't beat 'em, join 'em."

"You certainly did. I don't even know what to say."

"How about 'May the Force by with you'?" He winked.

"Sounds appropriate under the circumstances." I laughed.

He snapped his fingers. "Oh, what are you giving to the spectators tonight, by the way?"

"The usual cookies and cocoa. Why?"

"Send them my way after. I got this bucket of glow-in-the-dark lightsabers."

"I'm sure the kids will love those."

"See? I won't make kids cry anymore. That's gotta count for something, right? Perhaps it makes up for me being such a dick to you early on?"

"It might take a lot of lightsabers to make up for that," I teased.

We shared a laugh, and his eyes lingered on mine.

Feeling flustered, I looked back over at my house. "Well, I need to get started on the cookies and stuff. I'll be sure to send everyone across the street, although they'll probably come over here first. I don't know how anyone could resist getting a closer look at all this."

"Make sure you stop by, too. I'll save you a lightsaber."

"Okay." I laughed.

Later that evening, I thoroughly enjoyed watching from across the street as Cole's *Star Wars* display got the attention it deserved. He stayed dressed as Princess Leia the entire time. It was hysterical.

After the neighborhood visitors finally dissipated, I turned off my exterior lights and went inside. I hadn't gone over to Cole's. I guess a part of me still felt weird about initiating contact after he'd stood me up for dinner that night. *Let him come here if he wants to see me again.*

Several minutes later, I was just about to put on some tea when the doorbell rang.

I opened it to find Cole, no longer in costume. Instead, he wore a coat over a fitted black shirt and dark jeans.

"Well, if it isn't Princess Leia. I see you got tired of your garb."

"Yeah. I've been emasculated enough for one night." He laughed. "It was fun seeing all those smiling faces, though."

"You were a hit."

His breath was visible in the cold air as he asked, "Can I come in?"

"Of course." I stepped aside, allowing him to enter.

"It's so nice and warm in here, as always." He looked around, seeming a little tense. "So…I wanted to talk you…"

My ears perked up. "Okay…"

"That night when I canceled dinner—I wish I had come over." He looked down at his shoes. "I've regretted canceling ever since."

"Why didn't you come over?"

He took a deep breath and looked up. "I was hesitant to spend time alone with you because of how strongly attracted to you I am." He paused. "I mentioned before that you remind me of someone who hurt me. My ex cheated on me, and it's taken me a long time to learn to trust again. But it wasn't fair of me to buy into that negative association based on your looks. Not to mention, you're *way* more beautiful than she ever was—both inside and out." He smiled. "Bottom line, I didn't know how to handle my feelings, and I chickened out. But like I told you earlier, I'm done living in fear."

My heart raced. "I just assumed you weren't interested..."

"No. Just the opposite." He took a few steps closer. "In fact, nothing had interested me in a very long time until you came along. Just being in your house that one night took away my writing block. But it wasn't the house. It's you—the way I feel when I'm around you. Your sweet soul and beautiful spirit. You make me feel alive again."

His words took my breath away. "I never thought my grumpy neighbor would turn out to be the first person to make me feel alive in a long time, too."

His eyes went to my lips as he leaned in and took my mouth. I wrapped my arms around his neck and savored his taste as we fell into a deep and passionate kiss. My hands raked through his thick hair as our chests pressed together. It had been forever since I'd felt so turned on by a kiss, and my body buzzed with excitement. Somehow, I knew he wouldn't be returning across the street tonight.

After several minutes, we finally came up for air. I moved back to look at his gorgeous face. Then my eyes travelled down to his crotch and landed on the impressive erection straining through his jeans.

I raised one eyebrow. "Is that a lightsaber in your pants, or are you just happy to see me?"

His eyes sparkled. "That's no lightsaber."

Muffled noise registered from outside, drawing our attention to the living room window, which we were standing in front of. It seemed a few spectators had arrived late, probably hoping to see the lights. Instead, they'd watched us kissing.

Cole reached over to the lamp and clicked it off before pulling me back into his arms. "We seem to have lost power again." He spoke over my lips.

I smiled. "Oh, did we? That's a shame. Shall I get the generator?"

"No, ma'am. We're about to make enough electricity of our own to light up the block."

HOT ITEM

CHAPTER 1

Holly

"That's mine!"

"Really? Because I don't see your name on it, and it's in *my* hands."

I pointed to the cart next to me. "I was making room for it."

Ugh.

Figures.

Turning back, I got my first good look at the guy.

Dark hair, tanned skin in December when the rest of us look pasty, a chiseled jaw, and bright eyes that were annoyingly blue.

Gorgeous.

Of course.

And a jerk.

Aren't they all?

He peeked around me, and his brows shot up. "Is that all for one kid?"

"That's none of your business."

"Trust me. Your kid isn't going to miss this one toy with all that." He started to turn away and I just...no. *No.*

No. No! Five hours of shopping on Christmas Eve was enough to make the sanest of people snap, and I wasn't one of those to begin with. I lost it.

"Give me that!" I attempted to yank the box from the guy's hands, but he had too good of a grip on it. "I have been searching for that damn robot for weeks. You aren't going to just walk away with it when I had it first. *Give it to me!*" When he didn't relent, I started to scream—like a lunatic. "Security! *Security!* Someone help!"

The guy took a few steps back and held up his hands. "Did you forget to take your meds this morning, Ma'am?"

My eyes widened. *"Ma'am?* Did you just call me *Ma'am!*"

Security came running over. "What's going on here?"

I pointed to the guy. "He stole my toy, and now he just called me *Ma'am.* I'm thirty-one!"

The guard's brows pulled together. "You purchased that toy?"

"Well, no. I couldn't. Because he took it from me."

"So, he didn't *steal* the toy..."

"Well, he *stole* it out from under me! Tell him to give it back!"

"Ma'am...can you please keep your voice down."

Oh. My. God. "Can you stop calling me Ma'am, too!"

The guard put his hand on his walkie-talkie, which was holstered to his hip. "Ma'am." He shook his head. "I mean, Miss. You need to calm down, or I'm going to call the police."

"I will. As soon as you make him give that box to me."

The guard looked at the thief. "Sir, did you take that box from this woman?"

He shook his head. "It was sitting on the shelf, and I walked over and picked it up. She wasn't even touching it."

"Is it the only one or something?"

I answered. "It's the only one in the *state of New York*. I've been searching for it for *a month*."

The security guard pointed at the man. "I was speaking to him. What's your name, sir?"

"Bryce."

"*Pfft*." I rolled my eyes. "*Bryce*. Figures."

Bryce's brows dipped together. "What's wrong with my name?"

I waved my hand around at him. "It just goes with the whole package."

"The whole...package..."

"Yes, you know...handsome with a fancy name. You probably come from money, too. It's what gives you that sense of entitlement you so obviously have."

He looked at me incredulously. "You know, I appreciate women like you."

My hands went to my hips. "Oh really?"

Bryce shrugged. "Yeah, normally I meet a pretty woman, and she doesn't show me how nuts she is until *after* she knows where I live. It's nice of you to wear your insanity around your neck like a Christmas wreath. So all of us handsome, rich, fancy-named guys can keep our distance."

I scowled at him.

The poor security guard's head was bouncing back and forth between us like he was watching a ping-pong game. He took a deep breath and sighed.

"It's almost Christmas," he said. "Do you think one of you might find it in your heart to let the other have the toy? Maybe it will make you feel good on the inside."

I folded my arms across my chest. "Not me."

Good-looking Bryce mimicked my stance. "Not me, either."

The guard scratched his head. "I'll tell you what...can I have that box, sir?"

"Are you going to give it to her?"

"I'm going to bring it to the manager, and see if she can settle this dispute. I'm really not trained for this type of thing." He held his hands out, and Bryce reluctantly handed over the robot.

"Thank you. Why don't you two follow me?"

The three of us walked to the customer service desk, where a woman who looked as frayed as I felt listened to the security guard tell our story. She looked between us and sighed.

"So here are my choices. I can keep this thing behind the counter and no one gets it, or I can give it to whoever has the best Christmas spirit."

I pointed to my red sweater and cart full of toys. "Well, clearly that's me. I mean, look at him, he either just had a spray tan, or got off a plane from the Bahamas."

Bryce shook his head. "This is my natural skin color."

"Sure, it is."

The manager leaned both her elbows on the counter. "Listen, I don't have time for this. And Christmas spirit isn't about who buys more toys or looks more festive. It's about being kind to others and helping those in need. So I'll tell you what I'm going to do." She pointed to an empty folding table near the door. "We usually have a free wrapping service on Christmas Eve, but the two volunteers who were supposed to man the table came down with the flu, and I don't have any employees to spare. The volunteers wrap for tips, and all the money collected is donated to the local Toys for Tots. You two can work that table for the next few hours until we close at six, and whoever has more money in their tip jar to donate at the end of the day gets the robot."

I blinked a few times. "You can't be serious?"

She pointed to her stoic face. "Do I look like I have any sense of humor left?"

Bryce looked at his watch and frowned. "I'll do it."

The manager turned to me. "If only one of you wraps, that person is the default winner."

I glanced over at the table. "Can I at least get my own table so I don't have to sit with a thief?"

She shook her head. "Nope. That's what I got. One table. Take it or leave it."

I thought about what Mason's face would look like if he didn't get that robot tomorrow morning under the Christmas tree and sighed. "Fine. But he can't start without me, and I need ten minutes to make a call and get some coffee."

"Get something to eat while you're at it. You're gonna need all the energy you can get to wrap your way to the finish line." He winked.

I rolled my eyes, then walked away for a bit to call my sister, letting her know I was going to be late for Christmas Eve dinner at her house. Thankfully, Mason was already with her. She'd kept him after waiting in the two-hour line to see Santa early this morning so I could finish my shopping.

I grabbed a coffee just in the nick of time before the café closed early. On my way back to the department store, I was stewing. I'd earned that darn robot. I'd come here every day after work to see if they'd gotten any in. And finally today, smack dab in the middle of the shelf was a new one in the box. My eyes had landed on it first. Before his. I'd felt it was truly meant for me—until Blue Eyes snatched it.

Bryce was sitting on his side of the table when I returned.

"Are we ready to open?" he asked. "The manager gave me a sign to put up and two tip jars. Just say the word and we'll get rolling."

"Yeah. Fine," I huffed. "Do you even know how to wrap presents? Because I'm pretty good at it. So I'd be worried if I were you."

He shrugged. "I can't remember the last time I wrapped anything, actually."

"Then why don't you just give up this game?"

"Look...I made a promise to a little boy to try to get this damn robot, so I'm doing whatever it takes."

"You and me both."

As soon as we put the sign up, a few people started to line up to have their presents wrapped.

My first customer was an easy one, just a simple, square box. I took my time making the finished product look perfect.

The woman beamed after I handed it to her. "What a beautifully tied ribbon. Thank you so much." She left me a five-dollar bill.

Score.

"You're very welcome. Merry Christmas!" Smiling, I looked over at Bryce to find him struggling to wrap an oddly shaped cylindrical package. "Need some help with that?"

"Not if I have to fork over my tip." He laughed.

The older woman waiting for Bryce let out a frustrated breath.

Bryce kept trying to get the sides just right, but was failing miserably.

He finally handed her the most warped wrap job you'd ever laid eyes on and said, "Forgive my wrapping skills. I'm here to earn money for charity and trying to win a present for a special little kid. And...can I be honest?"

"Okay..." she said, not seeming very amused.

"I've been...a little distracted." He paused. "By your eyes."

What is he pulling?

She clutched the present to her chest. "My eyes?"

"Yeah. They're the most unique color of green I've ever seen. And I mean that in the best possible way. Sort of a... mix of gray, green, and gold." He grinned. "Stunning."

The woman pushed a piece of her hair behind her ear. "Well...thank you. I can't say anyone has ever told me that before."

"Shame, really."

"You know what?" She literally fanned herself, then said, "I'll just take this home and throw it in a bag I already have."

To my dismay, she then placed a twenty-dollar bill into Bryce's jar and strutted away looking like she had a new lease on life.

Twenty? I would never be able to catch up if this was his game.

Meanwhile my current customer had me wrapping a fake potted plant, which was a challenge to get right. And he left me a single buck.

After that guy left, I turned to Bryce and cracked, "I guess the only consolation of your swindling ways is that the money is going to charity."

"How am I swindling? That woman walked away happier than she was before she stopped here. She got something out of it. Win-win for everyone."

Except me, I suppose.

My son had asked for one thing this Christmas. *One thing.* And I couldn't deliver. Of course, it had to be the "hot item" of the season. But he really didn't ask for much year-round.

It's going to kill me to have to disappoint him if I can't make this work.

Relief washed over me to find that Bryce's next customer was a big, burly man. He wore a leather motorcycle vest and had some chains hanging from his jeans.

Good luck charming that one with your flirting, loverboy.

As I placed tape on a simple rectangular box while a teenager impatiently waited, I glanced over at Bryce as he struggled to wrap the man's teddy bear.

"Dude, I don't have all day," the guy groaned.

I chuckled.

Bryce apologized. "I'm really sorry. I'm new at this wrapping thing."

"Look. I don't mean to be a dick, but I'm late in picking up my son. I only have him tonight. Then I have to take him back to his mother's for Christmas with her and her new husband. It's hard enough competing with them, and now you're eating into my time with my son. So, I'm a little frustrated."

Bryce nodded. "Are you a single dad?"

"Yeah..." he muttered.

Bryce looked him in the eyes. "It's not easy, is it? My parents were divorced, too, and my dad did the best he could making his house a home for me. I wish I could go back and tell him that he didn't need to worry. That he was always enough for me. He didn't need to go over and above to constantly prove himself." Bryce handed the man the bear that had crinkled paper all around it and said, "If no one else tells you this, you heard it from me. You're doing a good job, sir. You're a good dad. And your son is lucky to have you."

Jesus. This behemoth man looked like he was about to cry like a baby. With red eyes, he took the misshapen package from Bryce before slapping a ten down on the table. He wiped his lids. "Thanks, man, I really needed that." He sniffled.

"My pleasure," Bryce said. "Have a Merry Christmas."

I shook my head as we watched the man walk away. There was a lull now with no one waiting in line on either side of the table.

"Mr. Disingenuous strikes again. I've got to give you credit. You can apparently pull anything out of your ass."

"Unlike my supposed attraction to the green-eyed woman, that was totally real. I meant every word," he said. "I could tell the guy was stressed, and deep down it had nothing to do with my wrap job." He turned to me, his eyes lingering on mine. "You know what? I can see the same stress and worry in you. You want nothing but the best for your son. That's why we're here in this dumb little competition."

"Yeah," I muttered, unable to argue with that. "Is it your son you're trying to get the toy for?"

"No. Just a boy I know who deserves it. I don't have kids."

"Oh."

"Are you married?" he asked.

I hesitated, then said, "My husband passed away a few years ago."

He frowned. "I'm sorry."

"Thank you."

He was silent for a bit, then said, "We never really properly met. Let's start over." He held out his hand. "I'm Bryce Holloway."

I took it. "I'm Holly."

"Holly Holloway." He chuckled.

"What?"

Did he just put our names together?

"The combination sounds like something a movie star would be named," he said.

"More like a small-town weather girl." I chuckled.

"Cornily fantastic name." He laughed. "What's your *actual* last name?"

"Johanssen."

"Swedish?"

"Yes."

"That explains the Nordic beauty."

It took me a few seconds to snap out of his vortex.

"You're doing it to me."

His brow lifted. "What?"

"Buttering me up. Probably trying to swindle the robot out of me, so I'll just hand it over to you along with my panties. Not gonna work."

Bryce bent his head back in laughter. "While I certainly would not refuse your panties, that wasn't where I was going with the compliment. Besides...look at my tip jar. Look at yours. I'm thinking you're the one who needs to start buttering *me* up, buttercup."

A little while later, a guy I'd hoped to never see again slithered up to the table.

"Holly? I thought that was you."

Ugh. I forced a smile. "Hi, Aaron."

"This is where you work now? You can't possibly be making the same dough I was paying you?"

"I actually don't work here. I'm sort of volunteering—wrapping for charity." I leaned to look around him, anxious to move on to the next customer, and pointed. "Do you...uhh...have something for me to wrap? Because there's a line behind you."

He grinned. "I got something for you to wrap alright..."

The leering tone caught Bryce's attention. He looked at Aaron and then me. Seeing *uncomfortable* written all over my face, Bryce handed the package he just finished wrapping to the customer and cleared his throat. "Can I help you with something, buddy? If you have something you want wrapped, I can take care of you."

Aaron's seedy grin widened. "I definitely would rather Holly *take care of me.*"

"I have to take the next person, Aaron. Have a good holiday."

Aaron leaned down. "You still got the same number? I'll call you."

I'd actually changed my cell phone number because of him. Yet I nodded. "Yep. Bye. *Next!*"

After the dirtbag moved along, Bryce leaned to me. "What's the story there?"

I blew out a puff of hot air as I shook my head. "Nothing really. He was my boss for a few months. I'd taken a second job for a while, waitressing on the weekends, and he was the manager. He's just...let's just say he didn't get the note that #MeToo was a thing."

Bryce's face hardened. "He touched you?"

"No, nothing like that. He just made me feel uncomfortable. He would always turn any conversation sexual. Sort of like when he just said he had *something for me to wrap*. And then, after I left, he kept texting me and asking me to go out. I actually changed my number to avoid him."

"That's harassment. It's illegal."

"Yeah." I shrugged. "I just quit as soon as I could. I'm a teacher, and a coaching position opened up, so luckily I didn't need the waitressing job anymore. To be honest, I wasn't very good at being a server anyway."

Bryce frowned, but nodded. "So what do you coach?"

"Bowling."

He smiled. "You're a good bowler?"

"I actually am. My parents divorced when I was seven, and my dad had visitation every other weekend and one day a week after school for a few hours. We did homework at the bowling alley while eating pizza and then bowled three games after."

"I've never been bowling."

"Really? How come?"

Bryce shrugged. "Not sure. I guess it was just not a sport my family was into."

"Oh..." I smirked. "Too blue collar for you?"

Bryce squinted, but his lip twitch gave away he wasn't really annoyed. For the next half hour or so, we had a steady stream of customers so we were both busy wrapping. The next time we had a lull in the line, I stretched my arms over my head.

"So what's your deal, Bryce? What do you do when you're not stealing toys from unsuspecting single moms, or schmoozing green-eyed old ladies?"

"I work in a family business."

I raised a brow. "Vague much? Is it the mafia or something?"

He chuckled. "No. If you must know, I was being ambiguous to avoid admitting you were right."

"Of course I was. But what was I right about?"

"Your comments. Earlier you'd said I was entitled because I probably come from money, and then what you said about bowling a little while ago. I'm not admitting I'm entitled, or that bowling is for blue-collar workers, but if I told you that my family owned a string of stores, it would just validate what you already thought of me and you'd gloat."

The biggest, most obnoxious smile spread across my face. "Your family owns a string of stores..."

Bryce rolled his eyes. "*Gloater.*"

"*Entitled.*"

The corners of his lip twitched again. "*Nut job.*"

I laughed. "Alright, so I *might* have come off a little crazy earlier. I'll give you that much. But you don't know what I've been through trying to get that damn toy. I spend an hour on websites every morning trying to find one online, and then I run here after school every day to see if any came back in stock. It's not easy being a single parent."

Bryce scanned my face, and his grew serious. "No, I'm sure it's not. Do you mind if I ask what happened to your son's dad?"

I sighed. "He was in a car accident. On Christmas morning, actually."

"Shit. I'm sorry."

"Thank you. It was four years ago. My son was just a toddler. Will went out to get some batteries for a toy that I'd bought our son—a toy that he wasn't even big enough to play with yet—and the police knocked on my door an hour later."

"Jesus, Holly. That's awful. And here I am being a jerk to you on Christmas Eve." Bryce raked a hand through his hair. "I can't even imagine how hard the holidays are for you."

I forced a smile. "Yeah, I think that's why I always overdo it for my son. I want him to have anything and everything since I can't give him the one thing he'd probably want more than anything." I felt myself getting emotional, which I didn't want to do, so I was relieved when a customer walked up to our table. She had a cart with a few items.

"I will give you the fattest tip if you can get these done in five minutes. I'm late to meet my boyfriend's parents for the first time."

The woman had been standing in front of Bryce, yet he waved her off and stood. "Holly here will have to take care of you. She's faster. Plus, I need to go to the men's room."

I don't know why, but I got the distinct feeling that Bryce had just bowed out so I could get the fat tip the woman had mentioned, and I had mixed feelings about that. Of course, I wanted to take home that stupid robot, but I also didn't want sympathy. So when he came back, I couldn't help but say something.

"I don't want to sound unappreciative, but if you just went to the bathroom so I could get that tip because you feel bad for me—I'd rather win on my own."

Bryce's eyes flickered to my lips before returning to meet mine. "Perhaps my motives weren't as altruistic as you might think..."

CHAPTER 2

Bryce

There was no way I could take that damn robot from her now that she'd told me her husband freaking died on Christmas.

I'd have to figure something else out for that little boy I'd promised to find one for. Maybe after Christmas it would be easier to snatch one up. A lot of people probably hoarded them, and someone was bound to return one. I'd come back and stand guard when the store opened the day after Christmas if I had to. Hopefully, he'd be okay with a belated gift. It's the thought that counts, right?

I could've just ended this now and told Holly I was going to give her the robot. But then she'd leave, and I might never see her again. I was enjoying getting to know her despite the crazy start we had. And let's be honest, I found myself insanely attracted to her. Her skin was so smooth, her blond hair like silk. Her eyes were a deep blue, the color of a dark ocean. And her body made me think thoughts that weren't appropriate to have about someone's mother. So, yeah, I decided to keep this game going a little while longer, even though I knew I was ultimately going to let her win.

My line was empty while Holly wrapped a simple tie box to my left. She had this habit of running her tongue along the corner of her mouth whenever she was concentrating. It was adorable and sexy at the same time.

I bit the bullet and asked, "Are you single, Holly?"

She placed a piece of tape on the corner of the box as she glanced over at me. "I haven't dated much since my husband died. Life is just too busy to really make the time." She tied a bow, then asked, "What about you?"

"I'm single, yeah."

"I know why I'm single, but what's going on with you?" she asked as she handed the box back to the man.

He dropped a dollar into her jar. When she frowned, I smiled, knowing that it no longer mattered what she earned. She'd already won and didn't know it.

"I'm picky, I guess." I finally answered honestly. "My mother would tell you I'm selective to a fault. But I don't think you can be too selective when it comes to a life partner. So, I'm in no rush."

A woman appeared, handing me a garden statue of some sort that seemed like it was going to be a nightmare to wrap. Another opportunity for me to look like a dumbass in front of Holly tonight.

She immediately took notice as I started out by cutting way too much paper.

"Want some help with this one?" She laughed.

"Are you sure you want to help the enemy?"

"In this case, it's going to honestly be painful to watch, so yeah." She winked.

I handed her the scissors and smiled. "Thanks."

When she took it, her petite hand brushed along mine, and I became more determined than ever to not leave here tonight without her number.

"Where is this little competition keeping you from being tonight?" she asked as she cut the paper in a straight line.

"My family's annual Christmas get-together. The favorite uncle and life of the party is just going to have to be fashionably late."

She cocked a brow. "Well, you're welcome to give up the fight and leave now."

"You'd like that, wouldn't you?"

The way I'd said that almost sounded...suggestive. I was having way too much fun with Holly, and it hit me that my prolonging this was actually keeping her from her family, which wasn't fair. *Jesus, Bryce. Can you be more selfish?*

I decided to concede now. Then I'd ask her out. In that order. I figured that was the correct chronology, since it was doubtful she'd agree to go out on a date with me if I was still trying to "steal" the toy.

A second after I'd had the thought, Holly's phone rang. She answered it, and that's when things went in a very different direction.

Her face turned white. "Oh my God, what?" She rushed up from her seat, clutching her chest.

I stood up, readying myself to help her if she needed it, even though I had no clue what the hell was going on.

"He's okay, though?" She paced. "Where did they take him?" Nodding repeatedly, she said, "Okay. I'm heading there right now."

She hung up, then rushed toward her seat to grab her coat and purse.

"What happened?"

"My son was sledding outside of my sister's house, and he had an accident. She said she thinks he's okay, but he did hit his head. They're taking him to the hospital as a precaution." Frenzied, she shook her head. "I'm sorry. I have to go."

I blinked. "Okay...uh..."

I didn't have a chance to respond because she ran off, her heels clicking against the ground as she disappeared into the distance. I couldn't blame her. But this sucked. The whole thing, but especially the fact that her son was injured.

My heart was still racing even a few minutes after she was long gone. I just sat there in a daze.

As a new customer approached the table, I immediately held my hand up. "Sorry. We have to close down for the night." I stood up and turned the sign around. "Merry Christmas."

I walked over to the customer-service desk where the woman was keeping the robot.

"Store will be closing soon. Do we have a winner?" she asked.

"Not exactly." I ran my hand through my hair. "Holly had to leave suddenly because her son had an accident. Sounds like he's probably okay but needed to be taken to the hospital as a precaution."

"Oh no." She covered her mouth with her hand.

"Yeah. He was sledding. Very scary. And on Christmas Eve, no less."

I could only imagine how she felt, having lost her husband on Christmas, the fears that must be running through her mind.

"What a terrible way to spend Christmas Eve," she said.

"Yeah." I sighed. "Anyway...I'm gonna take the toy. I only have her name. Gonna see if I can look up her address and drop the toy off to her so her son can have it on Christmas."

"I take it she won?"

"Yeah," I said in a daze, too tired to explain things any further than that. "I left the money over there in the tip jar. Someone should head over there before someone steals it."

"You got it." She grinned.

After I paid for the toy, I wished her a Merry Christmas and hit the road.

Back at my family's house, I greeted everyone, but soon after, disappeared into a quiet study to spend a few minutes Googling her name. Not one Holly Johanssen in her age range popped up in the entire Chicago area. I tried spelling Johanssen multiple ways, too. There was one listing for that name, but she was sixty-three years old. Nothing came up on social media, either.

That night, while I played along with my nieces and nephews, I was completely preoccupied, although I tried to stay as engaged as possible. The irony wasn't lost on me when my niece unwrapped a Christmas book, titled *Holly Jolly Tales*.

I felt like I'd somehow lost Cinderella, except I had no glass slipper. Nothing to go on to find her besides a name that seemed to be a dead end.

But after coming up empty in regards to Holly, I decided to go along with my original plan to drop the toy robot off at that little boy's house. At least someone will get the toy on Christmas. Maybe seeing his happy face would cheer me up.

I was really striking out today.

Pulling my hood up as I stood on the front porch, I looked around at the empty driveway and the street behind me. There were no cars anywhere, and not one light on inside the house. Not even the Christmas lights dangling from the roofline were lit. Snow had started to fall on my drive over, and a thin layer of white already coated the street and grass. Every fifteen seconds or so, a random gust of wind blew, making the tiny house resemble the inside of a snow globe.

I looked around for somewhere to leave the robot, but the porch only had a small awning, and snow already covered the ground below it. If this family didn't get home soon, the box and the toy inside would probably be ruined. It was seven o'clock now; maybe I could stop back in an hour if the snow wasn't too bad and see if anyone came home. It would really suck if this stupid robot went to waste.

Before today, I hadn't even known this thing was the popular toy for the season. It made me think about how my family had probably never gone through what Holly had—running around and trying to get the hot item so her son wouldn't be disappointed. My family could just pluck one from inventory before the toys even hit the shelves. Maybe there had been a little truth to what Holly had said earlier. What was it she'd called me today? *Entitled.* Yeah, that was it. Though, that thought only made me want to make sure this thing got into the hands of the little boy who I'd bought it for even more.

So rather than go home, I decided to stop by and visit my grandfather—the man who had made my cushy life so possible. It was after visiting hours, but I figured since it was Christmas Eve, the nursing home would probably be a little more lax than usual.

"Hey, Rena." One of the regular aides was at the front desk when I walked in.

"Hiya there, Bryce." She smiled warmly, and I held up a cardboard tray filled with hot chocolates and a box of munchkins from Dunkin' Donuts.

"I brought some hot chocolate and a snack."

She perked one brow. "Trying to bribe me so that you can sneak in after hours, are you?"

I grinned. "That depends. Will it work?"

She pointed her eyes down to the drink carrier. "Any of those have whipped cream?"

"They do."

She held her hands out. "He's in his room watching TV. Merry Christmas, Bryce."

"Thanks, Rena."

I found Pops all by himself, laughing out loud. The deep, baritone sound warmed my insides. As usual, he had on a full suit, vest and all, even though he was sitting in bed. "Hey, Pops."

He glanced over at me. "Are you the shoeshine boy?"

It made me sad that he didn't remember me anymore, but Pops wasn't hard to make happy, so I played along. "Sure am."

He looked down at his feet, and his forehead wrinkled. "Where the hell are my shoes?"

"I'll grab them for you. What color are you thinking with that suit? The brown or the black?"

He stared at me like I had two heads. "What moron would wear black with this?"

I smiled. "Brown it is."

Pops had a ton of clothes packed into the small closet in his room. The bottom of which was lined with old school wingtips. I took out a brown pair and pulled a chair up to the bed before helping him turn to face me.

We talked as I slipped on his shoes and took out the shoeshine kit that was always in his bedside table.

"I like a high shine." Pops pointed to his shoes. "So I can see my pretty face when I look down. Did you hear the one about the guy who gets his shoes shined and goes dancing at a club?"

I chuckled and shook my head. The human brain was pretty damn amazing. Pops couldn't remember that I was his grandson, but he could remember a shit ton of dirty jokes. I actually hadn't heard this one yet, but if he was telling it, I knew where this story was going.

"Nope, I don't think I've heard that one."

"Guy gets his shoes buffed so tight, they're like a mirror, and then goes to the club. He dances with the first woman, trying to impress her, and says '*I bet I know your favorite color.*' He looks down into his shiny shoe reflection and says, '*red.*' The woman is impressed. Little while later, he dances with a second woman...guesses her favorite color is blue. Then he dances with a third woman—looks down and grows perplexed. The woman notices and asks, '*What's the matter?*' He says, '*What color panties are you wearing?*' The woman responds, '*I'm not wearing any.*' Guy says, "*Oh thank God, I thought my new shoes were cracked.*"

The two of us laughed. When I was almost done with Pops' shoeshine, he said, "I'm going to open a store that sells suits someday. Good ones that fit right, imported from Italy. You should set up your stand outside. That'll be a gold mine for you...men who spend on a good suit don't like scuffed shoes."

I didn't have the heart to tell him that he *had* opened up a store that sold suits—and then another, then another, then another—and eventually they expanded from men's clothes to women's, then to children's. Today Kline's even carried makeup, home goods, and had a small section of toys, like the robot sitting in my car parked outside. "That's a great idea. I think I'll do that."

Even though Pops had appeared lucid for the last fifteen minutes, after I put away the shoeshine kit and came back from washing up, he looked over at me and asked, "Are you the shoeshine boy?"

I smiled sadly. "Yeah, I am."

Rena came by a little while later. Pops had lost interest in talking and was back to staring at the TV. "Bryce? I should be getting Mr. Kline changed for bed."

I nodded. "Okay, Rena."

I said goodbye to Pops and walked down the hall with Rena toward the exit. "How was your visit?" she asked.

"He thinks I'm the shoeshine boy."

Rena smiled. "That man can forget his own name, but he will never forget his style. He must've cut the women back in his day with how sharp he looked."

"Yeah, he was something else. Didn't matter if he was going to the supermarket, he wore his suit."

"Your sister came by earlier. She said you were over at one of the stores playing Santa. Is that true?"

I nodded. "Yeah. Every Christmas season Pops used to put on a Santa suit and beard and play Santa in one of his stores—taking pictures for the kids who came. He loved doing it. When he started to grow forgetful, and couldn't do it anymore, I filled in for him. I've done it the last eight years on Christmas Eve."

"The staff must get a kick out of that."

Sadly, unlike Pops, who everyone knew by name, most people didn't even recognize me as one of the owners of Kline's. I spent most of my time at the corporate office. But that anonymity worked for me today. No way would that manager have suggested Holly and I compete for the right to buy a robot if she had known who I was. Of course, I could've told her and walked out with the toy, but for some reason, I didn't. "They enjoyed it much more when Pops did it. He really got into character for it."

She smiled. "I bet he did."

At the door, I thanked Rena and told her I'd be back tomorrow to visit again. The snow was really starting to come down heavy now, so when I got into my car, I considered just going home. But then I looked over at the robot sitting on the passenger seat and thought about the little boy I'd met today. This thing would probably make his year...so what the hell, I'd go slow and try to make a kid smile on Christmas Eve, just like Pops would if he could.

CHAPTER 3

Holly

Some Christmas Eve this turned out to be. At least we were home.

After the doctors checked Mason out for any neurological damage, he got the all clear to leave the hospital. While he had hit his head crashing into a barrier, apparently there was no lasting damage. *Thank God.* I couldn't imagine something happening to my son; he was my entire world.

Rather than head back to my sister's so late, Mason and I headed home on the snowy roads to have a quiet, late Christmas Eve together. I'd let him stay up a little later tonight, and then after he went to bed, I'd play Santa and lay out all the gifts I had wrapped and hidden under my bed.

Unfortunately, the one gift he wanted wouldn't be under the tree. After everything he'd been through tonight, I wished he could've woken up to the surprise of the robot. I'd have to explain to him that Santa Claus promised to make a special trip back after Christmas to bring him one.

I had it all planned out. I would write a little note in "Santa's" writing and leave it next to the cookie crumbs that were left behind. My son always left cookies out for Santa, and I'd always enjoyed them as a midnight snack. Ever since my husband died, I'd used those little late-night moments to talk to him while I sat there alone, eating the cookies and staring at the lights on the tree. It had become my own private tradition. A sad one at that.

It was now 9:30, and Mason and I had just taken the cookies out of the oven. I'd told him he had to go to bed after we finished baking. The air filled with the smell of molten chocolate.

He jumped up and down. "Can I have one now?"

"We need to wait for them to cool first."

Several minutes later, Mason enjoyed three cookies with a tall glass of milk before we prepared a plate for Santa and left it on a small table next to the tree.

Then, I tucked my son into bed, hugging him a bit tighter than usual. To ensure he didn't wake up while I was placing the gifts under the tree, I always reminded him that Santa needed him to be asleep in order to safely come in unseen. It always baffled me how easily kids bought into the whole Santa Claus thing. I kept wondering when Mason would figure it out. He was seven, which was about the age that I discovered the truth. But I was happy it hadn't happened yet, because I was certainly in no rush to have him grow up.

Just as I'd finished the process of moving the presents from under my bed to the living room, the doorbell rang.

Adrenaline coursed through me. I hadn't been expecting anyone, and a horrible feeling of déjà vu hit as I remembered the police coming to my door to tell me that my husband had been killed in an accident.

My heart raced as I peeked through the peephole.

The man who met my eyes was perhaps the last person I ever expected.

It was Bryce, the gorgeous man from Kline's.

What?

And he was holding a large, wrapped box.

My heart pounded.

The robot?

How did he find me?

I opened as a rush of frigid wind hit me in the face.

"Bryce! How did you know where I lived?"

His eyes widened. Cold air billowed from his mouth as he just stood there for several seconds. Then he finally said, "You live here?"

"Yes. I can't believe you found me, and that you brought...the robot?"

"Yeah..." He blinked.

"I can't thank you enough. Did you feel sorry for me because of what happened? I don't know what to—"

"I can't believe this." He just kept shaking his head.

In my stunned state, I hadn't even invited him in from the cold. So I stepped aside. "Please. Come in. Just keep your voice low. My son is sleeping."

Bryce placed the wrapped present under the tree, then turned to me. "I hope the doorbell didn't wake him."

"He's a pretty heavy sleeper overall, and I don't hear him. So, I think we're good." I exhaled. "How on Earth did you find me?"

He looked a bit dazed. "Holly...I'm in total shock right now."

"Why?"

"I didn't think I was coming to see you. I thought I was dropping off the toy to the little boy I'd promised it to."

For a few seconds, I was totally confused. Until it started to click.

"Are you saying my son is the boy you were trying to win the robot for?"

"If he's Mason Gallagher at this address, yes." Bryce smiled. "He visited Santa Claus at Kline's earlier today, right?"

My eyeballs moved from side to side. "Yes. My sister took him."

He nodded. "I told you earlier my family owned a chain of stores. We own Kline's, actually. I left that little bit of info out. Every year, I volunteer to be Santa Claus on Christmas Eve. Today when I was in my suit, a little boy sat on my lap and told me how sad he was that his dad wasn't around on Christmas."

I covered my mouth. "Oh my God."

"He wasn't specific as to what happened, whether his father had died or was just not around. But it really hit me hard. I asked him what he wanted for Christmas this year, and he told me that he just wanted his mom to be happy, that it made him sad to see her cry over the holidays. That touched me even more, because most of the kids always have a list of material items at the ready when you ask them what they want."

Oh my heart.

"He's a special kid," I said.

"He insisted that he just wanted his mom to be happy again. I told him I really admired him for that. But because that's obviously not something I could promise him, I didn't quite know how to react. Before he left, I said to him, 'are you sure there isn't anything I can bring *you*?' And he was really funny. He said, 'well, if you *insist*...the only toy I really want this year is the TechBot.' He then blurted out his address, and I knew that I had to get it for him. But with so little time on Christmas Eve, I couldn't pull any strings. Whether I owned the store or not, there just weren't any left. So after I changed out of the Santa suit, I decided to check the shelves just to be sure. And that was when we met."

I looked up into his gorgeous baby blues. "I'm blown away. I don't even know what to say."

He shut his eyes momentarily. "I'm sorry. I was so shocked to see you that I didn't even ask how your son is doing?"

"He's fine, thankfully. No serious damage from the impact. We were lucky that the hospital wasn't too busy. We were cleared and discharged fairly quickly."

"I'm relieved to hear that." He blew out a breath. "I'd been looking for your contact information all night, ever since you left the store."

Scratching my head, I said, "Wait, I'm confused. If you didn't know I was Mason's mother, why were you looking for me?"

"After you told me about your husband dying on Christmas, I decided you deserved to win the robot. I made a decision to give it to you either way, but you left before I could tell you. I scoured the Internet for your name, and nothing came up in the area. I finally decided to go with the original plan, to give it to the boy from the store since I couldn't find you. I figured, at least that way, someone would get their Christmas wish."

My cheeks burned from embarrassment. "I'm a bit ashamed to say that I gave you a fake last name, Bryce. When you asked me...it was sort of right before the point where I started to trust you a little. I made a split-second decision, and it was the wrong one."

He nodded. "Okay, so you're not Holly *Johanssen*. That explains a lot."

"Johanssen was actually my grandmother's maiden name. But it's not mine."

"Holly is your actual name, though?"

"I can understand why you would doubt that, but yes, it is." I sighed. "And again, I'm so sorry for making that asinine decision."

"You're Holly Gallagher..." he said.

I smiled. "Yes."

"So, my Holly Holloway joke wasn't in vain, then."

I chuckled. "No."

"Well, that's good, at least."

I looked over at the robot he'd placed under the tree. "I just realized you wrapped that yourself."

"How did you know?"

"Because it's horrible." I started to laugh, but then suddenly tears sprung to my eyes out of nowhere.

"Did I upset you?" he asked.

"No." I wiped my eyes. "I'm pretty sure they're tears of joy. Because you've seriously made me so happy tonight."

"Well...I'm glad. Truly. You've been through a lot. It makes my entire Christmas to know that I could bring some happiness to your holiday."

A whiff of his delicious, manly scent wafted in my direction. There was no way I wanted to send this guy back out into the cold just yet.

"Do you have somewhere else to be?"

"I left my family party earlier, and probably won't be heading back. I was just gonna head home."

"Can I make you a cup of hot cocoa or something?"

His mouth spread into a smile. "I would seriously love that."

"Make yourself comfortable. I'll be right back."

A chill ran down my spine as I made my way to the kitchen. I had a hard time believing that things happen for a reason, especially after the way my husband died. What was the reason for that, you know? It was totally unfair and nonsensical. So, in general, I'd always felt the idea of fate was one big lie. But something about this night certainly *felt* like fate. What were the chances that my son and the boy he had encountered were one and the same?

When I returned to the living room, I asked, "I hope you like marshmallows?"

"I do. Thank you," he said as he took the mug from me.

I sat about a foot away from him on the couch and sipped my hot chocolate. "I'm sorry for running out the way I did," I said. "Once I realized Mason was fine and I had a moment to grab my bearings, I thought about you a lot tonight and really regretted the fact that I'd likely never see you again."

"Well, I guess we were meant to connect from the start. It's funny to think that even if our competition hadn't happened, I would've still shown up here tonight either way."

I grinned. "That's true, but I'm glad it happened this way. Because I might not have had the nerve to invite you in if I hadn't met you before now."

He put his mug down on the coffee table. "Can I ask you a personal question?"

"Yeah..."

"You said you haven't dated much since your husband died?"

I looked down into my cocoa and shook my head. "No, I haven't."

"Before you left, I was going to ask you out, but I also wondered if that was even something you would consider..." He grabbed his mug again and took a sip.

I finally looked up at him. "I don't want to be alone forever. I've considered getting back into the game. I do get...lonely." I immediately regretted being so honest. But for some reason, I felt like opening up tonight.

"If you don't mind my saying, it's a damn shame for a woman like you to ever feel lonely. After you left, I seriously couldn't think about anything else but your beautiful face."

Goosebumps prickled on the skin of my arms. "Thank you."

"If the accident hadn't happened and I had asked you out earlier, what would you have said—pending my giving up the robot fight, of course..."

I didn't really have to think much about my answer.

"I would have said yes, and then I would've told you my last name wasn't really Johanssen."

He smiled from behind his mug. "Good to know."

The lights from the tree reflected on his face, making Bryce's eyes sparkle.

I grabbed the plate of cookies from the small table next to the tree. "Would you like one? These are technically for Santa. But seeing as though you're basically him this year...you deserve the whole plate."

"I'll share them with you?" he said.

"Sure."

We sat in comfortable silence, devouring the plate of cookies. I'd told him to eat over the dish to intentionally drop some crumbs. Mason always looked forward to seeing Santa's remnants. It dawned on me that this was the first year since Will's death that I hadn't eaten these cookies alone in sadness. It felt good to have someone to share them with.

After we finished, Bryce suddenly stood up.

"I could stay here all night, Holly. I really love being around you. But I know you've had a long day. I'm sure you want to get some rest if your son is gonna wake up early. If he's anything like my nieces and nephews, he'll be up at the crack of dawn."

I *really* didn't want him to leave. But I also didn't want to tell him to stay because that might have seemed desperate. I thought of another approach to spending more time with him.

"What are you doing for breakfast tomorrow?"

He shrugged. "The elves and I were going to have Fruit Loops together, but I could totally ditch them."

"Would you want to stop by...to meet Mason? I'd explain to him that you're a friend. That way you can see him enjoying your gift."

"I would love to see you tomorrow, Holly, and meet him—formally."

"Say 9AM?"

"I'll be there with bells on—jingle bells, of course." He winked.

CHAPTER 4

Bryce

Despite the frigid air, my palms were sweaty as I stood in front of Holly's door on Christmas morning.

She opened and smiled, looking down at the massive box of Munchkins from Dunkin' Donuts in my hands. "You didn't have to bring anything."

"These are sort of my go-to thing that I bring whenever I'm a guest. And I know kids tend to love them."

"Oh, you better believe Mason is going to be thrilled."

The second I stepped inside, the boy came running into the room with his robot in hand.

"This is your friend, Mom?"

"Yes, this is Bryce," Holly said.

Mason waved. "Hello."

"Hey, buddy. It's really nice to meet you."

He looked up into my eyes and stared. "You...look familiar."

Uh-oh.

"Yeah, so do you," I answered, not knowing what else to say.

"This is my new robot. Santa brought him."

I feigned excitement and shock. "Is that a TechBot?"

"Yup."

"I can't imagine how lucky you had to be to get that. I heard it's the hot item of the season."

"I didn't think I would get one! Mom told me Santa might not be able to find it in time. I asked him for two things. This and for Mommy to be happy this Christmas. And she woke up this morning with a huge smile on her face. I got both things I wished for."

I turned to Holly and flashed her a mischievous smile. "Did she now?"

She blushed.

"Are those Munchkins?" he asked.

"They certainly are."

"I love them!"

"So I heard. There are lots of chocolate ones in there, too. Those are my favorite. Sometimes they skimp on those, but I made sure they didn't this time."

"Chocolate is my favorite. Thank you."

Mason was such a polite and grateful kid.

The three of us moved into the dining room. Holly poured me fresh coffee as we sat together at the table.

Everything was festive until Mason suddenly announced, "My dad used to take me to get Munchkins on Sundays."

I paused, then said, "I'm sure you must think of him every time you eat them."

"Every time." He looked down at his donut hole for a bit before he bit into it.

Noticing the sad look on her son's face, Holly attempted to lighten the mood. "Mason is participating in a winterfun run tomorrow in town."

I looked over at him. "You're running in the cold, eh?"

"Yup. It's gonna be so much fun, even though we're gonna freeze our butts off."

"You're a lot braver than me."

He grabbed another Munchkin and turned the tables onto me. "Who are you anyway? I mean...how did you meet my mom?"

Fair question.

"We met in a store, actually."

"Bryce's family owns Kline's," Holly added.

"I love that store! That's where I saw Santa."

I cleared my throat. "I'm so happy you have good memories there."

"You wanna come watch my race tomorrow?" he suddenly asked.

I looked over at Holly for guidance. "That's up to your mom."

She batted her lashes. "It would be nice to see you again, if you're free."

I actually did have plans tomorrow, but as of this moment? They were officially canceled.

"I'd love to go."

"Cool!" The boy got up suddenly from the table.

My head turned toward the entrance. "Where's he going?"

"Not sure. But I wish he would have excused himself first."

He came rushing back in and announced, "I know where I know you from now!"

My stomach sank, and I looked over at Holly, then back at him. "Where?"

He held out a book he'd been hiding behind his back. "You're on the cover of Mommy's book!"

Holly jumped out of her seat like a bat out of hell to snatch it from him. "Where did you get that?"

"You keep it in your bedside table. I found it the other day when I was looking for a tissue for my runny nose."

She'd snatched it so fast I didn't catch the full title, but the dude on the cover was shirtless, and all I saw was the word "alpha." *Damn.* That was what she liked, huh? I could be down with that.

"Hate to disappoint you, buddy, but that's not me." I chuckled.

"Really? It's not?" He giggled.

"I swear. It's not."

Holly literally placed the book under her ass on the chair, then warned, "Please don't be going into my drawers, Mason."

After he left to go play in his room, a few tense seconds passed before she turned to me.

"Well, that was super embarrassing."

"There's nothing to be embarrassed about. I like that you have an...open mind."

Her cheeks turned red.

"Can I see the book?" I teased.

"Not a chance in hell. That's why I'm sitting on it."

We eventually moved out to the living room and talked while Mason played with his toys. I told Holly a bit more about my family, going down the line of my siblings and naming all of my nieces and nephews. We discovered that we both grew up on the west side. So it was strange that we'd never encountered one another before.

At one point, she picked a small, wrapped gift from under the tree and handed it to me. "This is for you."

"Not fair. I didn't bring anything for you."

"Are you kidding? I still owe you for the robot. And once you see it, you're not going to be impressed. It's nothing. Just something I threw together this morning."

I ripped open the perfectly wrapped paper. It was a small box, and inside was a small, plastic tube-shaped contraption.

"I love it!" I laughed. "But...um, what is it?"

"It's a gift-wrap cutter. I noticed you were a little challenged with the scissors. This will glide right along the paper and cut a straight line. I had an extra one that was still in the package."

"Thank you. I'll cherish this and think of you when I use it. Although, in all likelihood, even without it, I doubt I'll ever wrap a present and *not* think of you."

"I sort of feel the same way."

As I looked into her eyes, I was feeling over the moon and just—grateful.

I can't wait.

I can't wait to get to know her better.

I can't wait to kiss her, to hopefully someday act out every fantasy in that little book of hers.

For the first time in a long time, I was truly looking forward to the new year.

She looked over at the clock. "We're supposed to be heading to my mother's for Christmas ham. We're already a little late."

I grabbed my coat and put it on. "No worries. I have to head to my sister's house anyway."

"So, we'll see you tomorrow for the run?"

I nodded. "Want me to scoop you guys up?"

"That would be nice."

"Cool."

She yelled out in the direction of her son's room. "Mason, come say goodbye to Bryce!"

The boy ran out, and instinctively I knelt down and opened my arms. Maybe that seemed a little forward for a first-time meeting with him, but technically I'd felt connected to him longer than that. He wrapped his arms around my neck and whispered in my ear, "Thank you for keeping your promise. I love it."

I froze as I slowly pulled away and looked him in the eyes.

Holy shit.

He knows.

He knew all along?

Then he mouthed, "Don't tell my mom."

I nodded, wanting to burst out into laughter. But I held it in.

He ran back to his room, and I looked over at Holly, who seemed to miss that entire exchange. I guess he had his reasons for wanting to milk the Santa thing as long as possible.

Holly then walked me out and shut the door behind her. We both lingered for a bit out in the cold. I wondered if she'd closed the door so that we'd have some privacy. I speculated that maybe that meant she expected me to kiss her. She couldn't comprehend just how badly I'd wanted to do that all day—or really from the moment I'd met her.

"Thank you for making this Christmas special."

I was honestly speechless. She was thanking *me*, when I felt like the lucky one here. I'd experienced so many feelings today, but perhaps the most unexpected was a feeling of gratitude mixed with a side of guilt for the opportunity to spend time with her. *With them.* Especially when *he* couldn't. And it wasn't fair. I hoped wherever he was, that he approved of this.

I promise I won't hurt her.

Apparently, Holly didn't get the memo that I was in the middle of a one-sided conversation with her dead husband. Because the next thing I knew, I felt her lips on mine. She'd gone in for the kill faster than I could blink. And I was so freaking here for this.

No wonder she'd closed the door.

I lifted her up and kissed her harder, falling more for her every second that she breathed into me. I went all in, sweeping my tongue into her mouth and savoring her sweet taste. When she moaned, I was a goner. After, I leaned my forehead against hers. We both had the goofiest smiles, and I couldn't help but think: Mason wasn't the only one who'd gotten his Christmas wish.

Santa had come through for *me*, too.

THE END

Happy Holidays to all of our readers!

OTHER BOOKS BY PENELOPE WARD & VI KEELAND

About Vi Keeland

Vi Keeland is a #1 *New York Times*, #1 *Wall Street Journal*, and *USA Today* Bestselling author. With millions of books sold, her titles are currently translated in twenty-seven languages and have appeared on bestseller lists in the US, Germany, Brazil, Bulgaria, and Hungary. Three of her short stories have been turned into films by Passionflix, and two of her books are currently optioned for movies. She resides in New York with her husband and their three children where she is living out her own happily ever after with the boy she met at age six.

Connect with Vi Keeland
Facebook Fan Group:
https://www.facebook.com/groups/ViKeelandFanGroup/
Facebook
https://www.facebook.com/pages/
Author-Vi-Keeland/435952616513958
TikTok
https://www.tiktok.com/@vikeeland
Website
http://www.vikeeland.com
Twitter
https://twitter.com/ViKeeland
Instagram
@Vi_Keeland
http://instagram.com/Vi_Keeland/

Other Books by Vi Keeland

ABOUT PENELOPE WARD

 **Penelope Ward** is a *New York Times*, *USA Today*, and #1 *Wall Street Journal* Bestselling author. With over two-million books sold, she's a 21-time New York Times bestseller. Her novels are published in over a dozen languages and can be found in bookstores around the world. Having grown up in Boston with five older brothers, she spent most of her twenties as a television news anchor, before switching to a more family-friendly career. She is the proud mother of a beautiful 17-year-old girl with autism and a 16-year-old boy. Penelope and her family reside in Rhode Island.

Connect with Penelope Ward:
Facebook Private Fan Group:
https://www.facebook.com/groups/PenelopesPeeps/
Facebook:
https://www.facebook.com/penelopewardauthor
Website:
http://www.penelopewardauthor.com
Twitter:
https://twitter.com/PenelopeAuthor
Instagram:
@penelopewardauthor
http://instagram.com/PenelopeWardAuthor/

OTHER BOOKS BY PENELOPE WARD

Moody
The Assignment
The Aristocrat
The Crush
The Anti-Boyfriend
Just One Year
The Day He Came Back
When August Ends
Love Online
Gentleman Nine
Drunk Dial
Mack Daddy
Stepbrother Dearest
Neighbor Dearest
RoomHate
Sins of Sevin
Jake Undone (Jake #1)
Jake Understood (Jake #2)
My Skylar
Gemini

Made in the USA
Middletown, DE
08 November 2022

14289981R00084